ODE TO MURDER

ODE TO MURDER

A LARKIN DAY MYSTERY
BOOK 1

NICOLE DIEKER

Cover design and interior design by Alan Lastufka.

First Edition published October 2022.

10 9 8 7 6 5 4 3 2 1

ISBN 978-1-7336919-5-6

For my parents, who taught me to
love both mysteries and music.

CHAPTER 1

"I'm not going to choir practice tonight," Larkin told her mother.

"Yes, you are," Josephine Day said, not looking up from her laptop. "I already told Ed you'd be there."

"You can't tell people I'll be places," Larkin said, not getting up from the sofa. "That's not how this is going to work."

"I think I get at least some say in how it's going to work," Josephine said. "Since you are living in my house."

"Temporarily," Larkin said.

"I'm well aware."

"And I'm supposed to be taking some time off," Larkin continued, shifting position just enough to activate her core and project her voice towards the kitchen table. "To think about what I want to do with the rest of my life."

"Are you thinking about it?"

"I'm thinking that I don't want to sing in community choir." Larkin was actually thinking that it had been a very long time since she had activated her core.

"It's not a community choir. We're bringing together all

of the choruses between Cedar Rapids and Iowa City. There will be singers from all over the Corridor." At least her mother had not called it the Creative Corridor this time, emphasis on *creative,* as if that would entice Larkin to get off the sofa and get back to creating. Larkin did not want to make art in Pratincola, Iowa. She didn't want to make art in any city where you had to say the name of the state afterwards.

Larkin didn't even know if what she did qualified as making art, anymore. At one point Larkin was very sure she was going to make art, staging plays and musicals that revealed truths no one in her audience had ever considered. At a different, slightly later point, she'd told herself it was just as worthwhile to teach other people how to make art—although she'd also asked herself how she could teach something she hadn't actually done. Larkin had considered this truth and then ignored it, not that it mattered. At this point, nobody was interested in hiring Larkin to teach or make anything.

"Are we getting paid?"

"Of course not."

"Then it's a community choir."

"It is a community *event,*" Josephine said, finally looking over the top of her laptop. Larkin was thirty-five years old; her mother's glare could make her feel thirteen again. "We are *celebrating.* Do you know how often orchestras perform Beethoven's Ninth?"

"Did you know before you looked it up online?" Now she was acting thirteen again, too.

"The Corridorchestra is going to be a very big deal for us, and I think you should participate." Josephine shifted her gaze back down to her laptop, and Larkin knew that meant her mother assumed the argument was over. That's how she would have staged it, back when she had assumed she would become a theater director at a university, a tenured faculty member, and the second Dr. Day. Instead, she was Dr. Day's daughter, on Dr. Day's sofa, watching Dr. Day return to academic administrata because her mother knew that Larkin was, in fact, going to choir practice tonight.

"Did you tell them I haven't sung in a choir since high school?"

"It's 'Ode to Joy,'" Larkin's mother said. "I think you'll know the tune."

———

Three hours later Larkin found herself thirteen pages into a thick green score, struggling to sight-read the alto line while mentally rehearsing various devastatingly clever ways to tell her mother that Beethoven's famous melody only took up a small portion of the last movement of the symphony. None of this was familiar, not to mention that it was in German—though right now they had been instructed to ignore the lyrics and sing the entire thing on "no." It felt exactly like what Larkin wanted to shout at her mother, at Ed the choral director who had waved at her like he already knew her, at her dissertation adviser who had suggested she take a break, at all of the department chairs at all of the interviews who had politely listened to her ask questions about their various campuses even though they all knew there was no chance in hell that she'd get hired.

Larkin glanced up at the framed portraits that hugged the speckled ceiling like a wallpaper border. The Cedar Rapids segment of what Ed had called the "megachoir" was in a church basement, because of course it was, and they were surrounded by visages of previous pastors who, as the decades proceeded, shifted from stiff lips to soft smiles, sepia to grayscale, male to female. All white, of course; Ed, wearing a T-shirt that read "this is my choir rehearsal shirt," was one of the few black people in the room.

And now Ed was looking at her because she'd lost her place. "Focus," he said, just like her mother and her dissertation adviser and everyone else in her life. The tiny towheaded woman sitting to Larkin's left, who had introduced herself as "Anni with an *I*" in the kind of voice that made Larkin suspect the *I* had a heart on top of it, quickly and quietly pointed at the correct part of the score. "Nooooooo," Larkin sang, sustaining the note and letting it crescendo.

At the break, while Larkin was reaching into her bag for her phone and hoping she could spend the next ten minutes learning about celebrities who had worse lives than hers, Ed walked right up to her metal folding chair and introduced himself. "I'm Ed Jackson," he said, holding out his hand. He was younger than Larkin had figured a man named Ed would be. Also jacked, which she wasn't expecting. She watched his bicep expand and contract as they shook hands. "I'm so glad you're here," Ed told her, and Larkin's eyes quickly went up to his face. "Your mother's said so many good things about you."

Larkin could no longer imagine what her mother said about her. *My daughter, who's in Los Angeles pursuing her PhD in theater* would have become *my daughter, who's working on her dissertation* and now *my daughter, who lives in my guest bedroom.* It didn't even have the decency of being her childhood bedroom; when Larkin was growing up, they'd lived in a bungalow that faced the Puget Sound.

But Dr. Day had wanted to be a college president, and was willing to move to Iowa to be a college dean, and when Anni-with-an-*I* said something about Dr. Ed being part of the Pratincola music faculty—"it's your third year, right?"—Larkin put it all together. She was in this church basement right now because her mother wanted her to do something besides take up the length of the living room sofa, and because Dr. Ed Jackson wanted her mother to approve his bid for tenure.

So Larkin stood up, because the folding chair was uncomfortable and because she was taller than Anni by two heads and taller than Dr. Ed by two inches. "I'm only here for a couple of months, really. But I'm glad I could help." Her theater training, as useless as it had turned out to be, had at least taught her how to tell a convincing lie.

"You have all of the information about the concerts, right?"

"Yes," Larkin said. Just because she hadn't looked at any of the information didn't mean she didn't have it. There would be one performance in Iowa City and one performance in Cedar Rapids, and at some point she'd put those dates on her currently empty calendar.

"I can help you get on the email list, if you want," Anni said.

Larkin *did not want*, but it didn't matter—Ed was already explaining to Anni how he'd gotten Larkin's email address from her mother, and Larkin was simply waiting until Ed and Anni paused long enough for her to excuse herself from this conversation. Up the stairs, past the line of women waiting to use the restroom, and out the door.

It was still light out, and still warm; a cluster of gnats hovered in front of the glowing church sign and the air felt like the city had just taken a shower. Easy for Larkin to forget that it was September; that everyone was back in school except for her.

"Want a light?" It was the accompanist; salt-and-pepper hair, rolled shirtsleeves, leather satchel slung across a slim chest. Slender fingers holding out a lighter. The cigarette was in his other hand; when Larkin looked up, she saw him looking her both up and down.

"I don't smoke."

"So you're just out here to enjoy the night air." He took a drag off his cigarette; exhaled. "I'm Harrison," he said, putting his lighter into his satchel and offering his hand.

"Larkin." They shook, and then Harrison reached into his satchel again. "Don't tell anyone," he told her, as he unscrewed the top of a battered flask.

"I don't know anyone," Larkin said, watching him drink and then shaking her head as he held the flask in her direction.

"I thought I hadn't seen you before," Harrison said, and Larkin saw his body tense just enough to reveal the truth; he was well aware that he hadn't seen her before, and was pretending to be casual. Still, he was doing a good job of it. Larkin didn't often get the chance to flirt with people. She had her father's height and her mother's hips, which seemed to ward off the majority of men; plus, as a theater director and graduate student she had been exceptionally sensitive to the power dynamics, unethicality, and general ickiness involved in pursuing a relationship with anyone in her cast or crew or classroom or cohort, male or female. So she'd enjoy this opportunity, even if Harrison was a little old for her.

Larkin smiled, with subtext. "I suppose I'm new in town."

"Which town?"

"Pratincola."

"Ah," Harrison said. "Home of the Fighting Roses."

"They have thorns," Larkin said. She had seen as much, from the banners strung around her mother's college. Her mother had explained that it was a small, liberal arts school; while the students themselves were sharp, the football team was lucky to win one game per season.

"Pratincola was the big city, when I was growing up," Harrison said. "It had a coffee shop."

"Now it's got everything," Larkin said. "Or so my mother tells me." She instantly regretted bringing her mother into the conversation; it felt like the antithesis of flirting. She followed up with the kind of coy banality that would make herself sound mysterious and Harrison sound clever. "But you already figured out that I'm not from around here." Larkin wished she had an excuse to shake her long, dark hair out of its last-minute ponytail, but that would be the kind of staging that she would describe as *a gesture overused to the point at which its symbolic meaning prevents the audience from experiencing the truth of the moment*—the academic way of saying *cliché*—if someone else did it. She let her weight shift onto one leg instead, angling her torso and positioning herself to share the scene.

"Where are you from, Larkin?"

It had been years since Larkin had known how to answer this question. "Los Angeles," she said. "New York. Minneapolis, for six months. Cambridge"—which had also been for six months, but she left that part out—"and Portland and Seattle." She'd actually grown up south of Seattle, in Tacoma, which meant that she had just listed six cities without naming the one that most people would consider the correct answer to "where are you from," but she figured nobody in Eastern Iowa would know where Tacoma was. She hadn't known where Pratincola was until her mother moved there.

"A rolling stone," Harrison said. "I admire it. Sometimes I wish I'd lived in a few more places." He glanced at Larkin again, eyes crinkling to match his smile. "I suppose there's still time." Then he glanced at his watch: silver, not smart. "Speaking of which—"

"We should go."

"Yes," Harrison said, stubbing out his cigarette under a scuffed leather shoe, adjusting his satchel, and opening the church door. "Oh, joy."

———

Over the next week, mostly to spite her mother, Larkin only left the house to go to choir rehearsal. If it wasn't Thursday evening or Sunday afternoon, she stayed indoors and under the air conditioning vent; outside felt like walking through one of the thick, chewy brownie mug cakes Larkin kept microwaving for herself, shaking a mug's worth of brownie mix out of the box at a time. When Josephine suggested that Larkin go pick up some groceries, Larkin downloaded an app and ordered them online. When Josephine asked if Larkin had gotten a chance to check out the library yet, Larkin said that she could still use her Los Angeles library card to check out e-books—"and I bet they have a better selection." When Josephine asked if Larkin was making new friends in the choir, Larkin said "Well, some old lady named Marlene baked us all scotcheroos, which is apparently what this town calls chocolate-covered Rice Krispies treats, which is what I called them, and I'm pretty sure she hates me now."

"No one could hate you," her mother replied, the two of them at their usual spots; Larkin with her phone on the sofa and Josephine with her laptop at the kitchen table. "You're so *pleasant*."

There was silence, for a moment, and then Larkin's

mother spoke again. "There's also butterscotch," she said. "In a scotcheroo. And peanut butter."

"Okay, Mom."

"I'm just saying—"

"I know," Larkin said. Her mother had *just said it* often enough. "Pay attention to the details."

"Well, they're important," Josephine said. Her specialty, before it was administration, had been poetry; she had no patience for any Shakespeare production where the actors spoke the language naturally, and loved telling her students—and her daughter—that *the feelings were carried on the feet*. Dr. Day was all about feet and meter and iamb and caesura; she'd never had to worry about making art because she'd been so good at explaining what it was made of.

"Especially in a place like Pratincola," her mother continued, still explaining. "The way you treat people, the way you behave—people remember. For years, sometimes."

"You're not doing a very good sales job, Mom."

"I love it here," Josephine said. "It'd be nice if you tried to like it."

"I don't have to like it," Larkin said. "I have to get my life together."

"Fine," Larkin's mother said. "Then get your life together. Did you get any work done today?"

"Yes," Larkin said, because she had spent roughly fifteen minutes looking at open faculty positions that she no longer considered herself qualified to pursue, and then spent roughly fifteen seconds asking herself what kind of job she could get with a resume that included four years of theater and food service gigs followed by five years of graduate school and two years of—well, the past two years could be explained, everyone would understand that story. Then Larkin had opened her bank app to see the number that represented her checking account balance, closed it before she could see the numbers that represented her student loan and credit card debt, and spent the rest of the afternoon watching Baz Luhrmann's *Romeo + Juliet* on her phone. Her mother was wrong about Shakespeare, which meant she could be wrong about anything.

"I'm not going to stay here forever," Larkin said, staring at the sofa.

"I never said you would," her mother said, looking at her laptop.

"I'm going to finish my dissertation and then leave," Larkin said, but although she put plenty of dramatic emphasis into the words, she was fairly sure that her audience didn't believe her.

CHAPTER 2

Larkin was almost late to Thursday's rehearsal because she hadn't paid attention to the details; she drove to Cedar Rapids, noticed the church parking lot was empty, and then pulled out her phone to check the three choir-related emails she had received that week, none of which she had read carefully, all of which reminded her that rehearsal would now take place at the orchestra hall. "First time with the megachoir!" Ed had written. "I hope you're all practicing at home. We don't want those Iowa City singers to show us up!"

Larkin was not practicing at home. It wasn't her home, for starters. Nor was it, apparently, her day—but she pulled a sloppy U-turn in the empty parking lot and drove ten blocks west. The one good thing about living in the Creative Corridor was that it didn't take much time to get between places. If she had still been in Los Angeles, she would have had to text whoever was responsible for taking attendance to let them know that by the time she got on the 405 and made it down to Culver City, the rehearsal would probably be over.

When Larkin got out of her car and began walking towards the restored Art Deco performance space, the windows of which were currently plastered with posters advertising not only Beethoven's Ninth but also three musicals, two string quartets, one ballet, and a band called the Pork Tornadoes, she heard a voice behind her: "You're going the wrong way!"

It was coming from a young woman, corn-fed and honey-haired, wearing a sleeveless shift and sandals. "I saw you holding your score," the woman said, by way of explanation. "You can't go in the front; we have to go in the stage door."

Of course they would. Larkin should have known that. This was her world, or it was supposed to have been. Now it was this other woman's world, as she quickly learned; Jessalyn Barnes was the soprano soloist, and was arriving a few minutes late because she taught voice lessons on Sunday afternoons—"but it's okay, Dr. Ed knows"—in addition to her adjunct professor gig at one of the six billion small Midwestern colleges that all seemed to be within a two-hour drive. It was the kind of job Larkin swore she would never take, back when she still thought she'd have a choice. Low paying, in the middle of nowhere, never knowing whether you'd be hired on for the next semester. Now she couldn't get a miserable little adjunct gig if she tried—and she had tried. Which meant that Larkin found herself uncomfortably envying Jessalyn, who was younger, better looking, better dressed, more credentialed, gainfully employed, *and* a soprano. Larkin's voice had descended from soprano to alto during adolescence, and she had never forgiven it.

"Don't say that," Jessalyn said, when Larkin made the quip aloud. "I tell my students you've got to embrace your own voice, not wish you had someone else's." She dropped hers into a whisper as they approached the stage. "And there's so much good alto repertoire out there. You could sing Dido! *When I am laid, am laid in earth. . .*"

The rehearsal had just started when Larkin and Jessalyn arrived, and although Larkin had hoped to blend into the 150-person megachoir without being noticed, she saw that Anni had not only saved her a seat but was now eagerly beckoning her to claim it. This meant that Ed, and everyone else, had to watch her squeeze her long and not-particularly-thin legs past several sets of knees.

"Good to see you, Larkin," Ed said. Larkin would have been sharper about it, if she had been directing; this must be that Iowa Friendly she'd heard so much about. Then he got down to business. "So. . . German! What do we know about German?"

He looked over his choir, chose someone with his eyes, and they responded: "Ds are Ts!"

"Yes!" Ed said. "*Und* is pronounced *unt*. But not *oont*. It's a different vowel. Are my IPA people in the house?"

A handful of Midwestern *woo-hoos!* confirmed that the IPA people were, in fact, in the house. Larkin had not studied the International Phonetic Alphabet in either college or grad school, even though she'd had the chance. The IPA was for pretty girls like Jessalyn, who were destined to be actors and vocal coaches and soprano soloists; Larkin, who had always been told she could be pretty if she tried, had also been told (at her first-year undergrad assessment) that she should consider dramaturgy or directing.

Larkin had thought that the one good thing about having to move to Iowa and live with her mother was that she wouldn't be surrounded by all of that anymore. She wouldn't have to walk through a stage door or listen to people go on about *schwa* sounds. She wouldn't have to feel too tall and too awkward next to people like Jessalyn who always got the spotlight and didn't even have the decency to be a jerk about it. Larkin had been an assistant director in New York. She had spent the past seven years studying and working in Los Angeles. She had assumed that in Iowa she would, at least, be the smartest person in the room.

But she didn't even know the IPA, and all of these Eastern Iowans did.

Which meant that when they split up into sections to play getting-to-know-you games, after filling paper plates with cookies and other home-baked goodies that several choir members seemed to have brought with them on principle—Larkin stood in the shortest line, grabbed a scotcheroo that did not taste like it had peanut butter in it, and thought about all the snarky ways she would inform her mother that she had in fact *paid attention to the details*— she glommed onto Anni because she didn't know anyone else's name and then immediately insulted her.

It was an accident, really. If Larkin had thought before she spoke, she would never have said it, but they were going around the circle and answering questions they literally pulled out of a Hawkeyes ball cap, and Anni's question was *if you could go anywhere in the world, where would it be?*

Her answer was "There's this cruise, it's mostly a nerd cruise, we do math and things, there's also music, but it's nerd music, some people play Dungeons and Dragons, I've been ten times."

"That doesn't count." The words were out before Larkin realized, though she knew exactly why she'd said them: to make herself look good and make Anni look foolish. "You could go *anywhere in the world*. Pick somewhere new."

Anni looked back at Larkin, her eyebrows raised over her round-framed glasses. "But we go to new ports of call every year."

Larkin couldn't tell if Anni had registered the insult. Another woman—gray-haired, brought the scotcheroos, *Marlene*—definitely had. Marlene glared at Larkin, and so when Larkin drew her card, which asked her to share the most famous person she'd ever met, Larkin didn't say anything about getting to study with Anne Bogart or assisting on a play that starred Benedict Cumberbatch. Instead, she said: "Cookie Monster. Mom took me to see *Sesame Street on Ice* when I was three."

That wasn't even the truth. It was her dad who had taken her. But the one question Larkin hated more than "where are you from?" was "where's your father?" So she decided not to put herself in a position where she'd have to answer it. Not yet, anyway.

The four soloists—Ben the baritone, Gerald the tenor, Shawnta the alto, and Jessalyn the soprano, *see, Mom?*—were not part of the getting-to-know-you games; they were clustered around the Steinway discussing something with Dr. Ed. When they were finished, Jessalyn and Gerald went straight for the snack tables; as they passed the circle of altos, they heard Jessalyn ask, "who's playing these rehearsals?"

"Harrison," Anni said, twisting over the back of the seat with the answer, even though the question had not been asked of her. "He'll be coming in for the second half, now that we're done learning the German."

When Larkin had studied with Anne Bogart, the experimental theater and opera director who was the kind of famous that only theater people would appreciate, she had learned a system of analyzing human interaction called Viewpoints. The theory was that you could understand a person, as well as the relationship between two people or the relationships among a group of people, by exploring the ways they positioned themselves in a room, the shapes they made with their bodies, and so on. Larkin's favorite Viewpoint was called *kinesthetic response*; it was a way of looking at how a single movement or statement rippled, physically and emotionally, through a group of characters.

So she looked, and saw that Gerald was annoyed with Anni's interruption; that Anni's eagerness to provide it faded when she saw Gerald's face; that Jessalyn had frozen, for an instant, before looking over the circle to match eyes with Marlene—who, as usual, looked like she wanted to punch someone. Her hands, which had previously been holding her purse in place on her lap, now tightened into fists. This made her purse start to slip down her knees, so she grabbed it back into place, breaking eye contact with Jessalyn, who glanced down at the paper plate she was holding, picked up a lemon bar, and bit off the end. A tiny cloud of powdered sugar.

"They're still using Harrison?" Gerald said. "He's a drunk."

"He's good, though." That was from Anni. "They get him to play everything."

"Well," Jessalyn said, and then didn't say anything else. Her lemon bar had red lipstick at the bite mark. She and Gerald moved on, and the moment was over.

"I hope we're not done learning the German," Marlene said, her hands tensed and her voice cheerful. "I don't think I know it at all."

But they were, at least for the evening, and Harrison arrived as they were shuffling their chairs from circles back into rows. He put his leather satchel on the Steinway's closed lid, swiveled the knobs at the bench, and ran through a flashy piano riff that Larkin was sure she recognized—from *Sesame Street,* coincidentally enough—but couldn't name.

"All right, Harrison," Ed said, stepping back onto the podium. "That's enough Liszt. Let's dig into some Beethoven! How about we start from the beginning and see how it goes? Soloists, would you please stand?"

They stood; Ed conducted; Harrison played. Ben the baritone was the first to sing, Beethoven's familiar melody filling the auditorium as the megachoir echoed his claim that Freud should get funky, or whatever *Freude, schöner Götterfunken* meant. Then the alto, tenor, and baritone soloists sang a more show-offy version of the "Ode to Joy" theme, with the soprano—well, the soprano was supposed to join in, Larkin knew enough about music to follow along in her score, but Jessalyn missed her entrance.

Ed stopped them. "Want to try that again, from the quartet?" No comment on anything anyone had done wrong, just a chance to start over. This time Jessalyn came in at the right time, but as her voice soared towards the high A, it suddenly faltered. Ed kept going, bringing in the full choir for a recap of the famous tune before letting the soloists take off on what Larkin admitted were some glorious vocal runs, the kind of thing you spent your whole life learning how to do before realizing that there were hundreds of other people who had spent their lives doing the exact same thing, and while she was thinking about how unfair it was that the performing arts world trained so many people to be so particularly skilled and then only ever let a few of them do it for a living, Ed stopped the soloists again.

"Jessalyn, are you okay? I'm losing you in the mix."

"It's not my best day," Jessalyn said. "I'm sorry."

"You've been teaching all afternoon, right? That's rough on the voice." Ed smiled at her. "Do you have enough in the tank to run it through? Then I can let the four of you go and focus on the choir."

"Sure," Jessalyn said, and she smiled back, and then Harrison spoke up. "Jess. You need to repeat that F sharp in measure 307. You're singing it like the two previous measures, but it's different. Here, listen." He played the soprano line as 150 people watched and waited, which meant that 150 people saw Jessalyn start crying.

"All right, megachoir!" Ed said, turning back to the chorus and taking control of the room. Jessalyn was digging awkwardly into her purse, holding various items in the crook of her arm until she found a packet of tissues. "We're going to start at measure 313. Harrison, give them their pitches. Soloists, you can take a seat for now but Gerald, I want you to be ready at the allegro."

They sang; Gerald sang; Shawnta put her arm around Jessalyn's shoulders. The soloists were dismissed as soon as they made it to the end of the movement, as promised; the rest of them stayed for another hour, working entrances and cutoffs. After a little speech about how they'd done "great work today" and should make sure to "listen to the recording I sent you" (in an email Larkin had already archived), Ed asked them to please help stack the chairs. That would have been an assistant stage manager's job, in Larkin's world; here, it turned out to be everybody's—though Anni took care of Larkin's contribution. "It goes faster if we take two," Anni explained, stacking both of their chairs and hoisting them towards the back of the stage.

That left Larkin free to leave, which was fine with her. As she walked down the dimly lit hallway, covered in cinderblock autographs and posters from previous performances, towards the stage door, she heard footsteps echoing hers. She turned her head without stopping her stride, out of New-York-and-Los-Angeles reflex. It was Harrison.

"How did you enjoy the megachoir?" he asked, as he caught up. "I don't know why Ed doesn't call it the Corridorus. Pairs better with Corridorchestra, right?"

"Sounds like a dinosaur," Larkin said. It was the best she could come up with after four hours of rehearsal.

"Maybe that's it. He doesn't want to insult the actual dinosaurs in the group." They reached the door; Harrison immediately reached into his satchel for a cigarette. "Jess has got to get her act together," he said, as they continued walking towards their respective cars. "That cute little music teacher schtick is only going to get her so far."

You and Jessalyn were a thing, Larkin wanted to say. To get it out into the oppressive, sticky air. Instead, she said "Yeah, for sure," and clicked the fob to unlock her car.

"California plates," Harrison said. "I would love to hear that story."

"I'd love to tell it to you." She paused, not opening the car door. The next move was his.

"How about we go get a drink sometime?" Harrison dug into his satchel and took out a palm-sized notebook. "Write down your number. I know, I'm the last living person who doesn't have a smartphone. At this point I'm hoping it makes me look cool."

Larkin took the book, wrote her number, handed it back. Their fingers brushed, lingered, released. For an instant Larkin wondered if Harrison was going to kiss her, the two of them standing in the bike lane next to Larkin's car—but then they heard voices, the rest of the megachoir done with their chairs and ready to go home, and all Harrison said was, "I'll call you."

And Larkin, as she drove back to her mother's home, decided that she was no longer jealous of Jessalyn.

CHAPTER 3

Larkin checked her phone again, even though she knew that it would be extremely unlikely for Harrison to call her fifteen minutes before rehearsal when he hadn't called her all week. Sunday's rehearsal had been just for the soloists, so it had been a full seven days since she had last spoken to Harrison—and Larkin shoved her phone back into her pocket before pulling off the *Hamilton* T-shirt that she had pulled out of one of the still-unpacked boxes that she had unstacked from the walls of her mother's guest bedroom because she needed something to wear to show Harrison how beautiful she was *and* how angry, and it wasn't the wrinkled floral blouse that she didn't know why she still owned, and it wasn't the pink tank top with "theater kid" spelled out in glittery rhinestones, and it wasn't the *Hamilton* T-shirt, even though hers was from the original Broadway production, not one of the touring ones. She and a group of friends had flown from Los Angeles to New York, adding both miles and debt to her credit card.

But she wouldn't think about that. She had told herself not to think about any of her debts, whether they were owed to the credit card companies or to the student loan companies, until after she finished her dissertation and gotten herself out of forbearance. Of course, Larkin had also told herself not to think about when Harrison would call, and then whether he would call, and then why he hadn't called.

She couldn't get away with wearing a dress to rehearsal, could she? Larkin didn't wear dresses often, but she had a little black number in one of these boxes somewhere. What she didn't have was time—so she ended up throwing on the same gray tee she had been wearing earlier that day, because *who cared, he hadn't called*, and then found herself quickly applying last-minute red lipstick in the car, tilting her face so she could see her lips in the rearview mirror, before running towards the stage door.

She was just early enough that nobody noticed her entrance—except Anni, of course. Larkin said "fine, how are you" and "yeah, it is hot out" and "you're right, I guess it is the first day of fall" while watching for Harrison, who had to be in the theater somewhere because his bag was on the top of the piano. He was not anywhere in the room, and then there he was, walking past the assembling singers to talk to Ed, which was fine, and then sitting down at his piano bench, which was fine, and then not scanning the room for Larkin, which was *not fine*. He should be looking for her, at least out of apology. But Harrison looked at Ed and he looked at Jessalyn and he looked at Ben and Gerald and Shawnta. Then he looked at his music.

"I like your hair," Anni said. Larkin had blown it dry and worn it down.

"Thanks." Anni's hair was short, an untidy pixie. She was wearing the same outfit she'd worn to every previous rehearsal so far: a blue-and-white striped shirt paired with the kind of pants that only revealed themselves to be leggings if you looked closely and the kind of shoes that only revealed themselves to be sneakers if you looked even closer. Her shirt, which appeared to be some kind of linen blend, was impossibly unwrinkled; Larkin's last-minute tee had seatbelt sweat stains across the front and she'd only been in the car for five minutes.

"All right, let's get started. We're at 595, the andante maestoso." Larkin could tell that Ed was trying to shift into Serious Director Mode. They had four rehearsals, counting this one, before the performance—three as a megachoir, and one dress rehearsal with the orchestra. Today's rehearsal would be nit-picky and boring and everyone would lose focus and then Ed would lecture them on how they needed to stay focused. She'd led these kinds of rehearsals before. She hated them.

"Let's stop." They were a measure in. "Men, I'm hearing some of you put a *t* sound at the beginning of *seid*. It's a *z* sound, not *tz*. Can you hear the difference? Ben, sing it for them."

Ben sang, the men tried to sing, Ed stopped them again. This kept going, phrase after phrase, even though it didn't matter. Nobody would care if a couple of men sang *tzeit* instead of *zeit*. They could sing *Fahrvergnügen* and the audience probably wouldn't even notice. Larkin knew how many things you could get away with in the theater, in plain sight. Musicians never seemed to understand this.

In this case, Larkin chose to get away with watching Harrison's hands instead of Ed's; the hands she had imagined doing all kinds of things that were not safe for rehearsal, she couldn't keep her *Gutens* and *Bösens* straight while thinking about Harrison stroking and caressing and entering—and then simply *entering numbers into a phone*, that is what he had to do to make all the rest of it happen, and that is what he had not done. So he would have to tell her why, when they took their first ten-minute break, except he did not do that either. Harrison got up, got his bag, got a snack off one of the tables, and got himself off the stage without once looking Larkin's way. It seemed impossible that he wouldn't give her at least a glance, given that Larkin had not stopped looking at him until he was literally out of sight.

But he hadn't, just like he hadn't called, and Larkin almost got up to follow him, but didn't. She didn't want to end up like Jessalyn, crying over spilt dicks. So she waited in the line at the restroom, waited in the line at the cookie table, grabbed a cookie from a stack labeled "Monster AF" because she still had a sense of humor, and sat by herself in the alto section until the break was finally over.

Because it had gone long, much longer than ten minutes, and Ed had shifted from serious to perturbed. "Has anyone seen Harrison?" Larkin watched a ripple of headshakes, a murmur of *no*s. "All right," Ed said, as if saying it would make it so. "We can't waste any more time. Anni, can you play?"

Anni leapt up, score clutched to her chest, out of the aisle and at the Steinway before her "Yes!" had reached the back of the house. "Take your time," Ed told her, the hint of a smile spoiling his Serious Director face—Larkin knew he couldn't keep it up—and Anni quickly adjusted her bench and cracked the spine of her score so it would lay flat. "We're going to take it from the top," Ed said, and they did.

The whole space felt different, now that Anni was at the piano. She was not the showy, nuanced pianist that

Harrison had been, but she was competent. More than competent—she was happy, her eyes bouncing between Ed and her music and her hands and back again. Ben picked up her energy and carried it into his baritone solo; when the choir followed with their entrance, Larkin thought that this was the first time the piece had actually sounded like an ode to joy.

And then Ed stopped them.

"Tenors, you weren't ready for that." This was the kind of directing Larkin hated. They'd gotten the emotion right, so why get all fussy about the entrance? "I need you all to stay focused," Ed continued. "I know it's a long day."

They began again. They stopped. They repeated, and continued, and stopped, and Ed told them once again to stay focused, and then he very nearly raised his voice when he tried to start them again and nobody knew where they were because they'd started and stopped so many times. Larkin had by now realized that the only reason she knew any of her music was because Anni had been singing in her ear, and now that Anni was at the piano she had no one to follow along with, and she didn't know the German, and when she sang *welt* instead of *velt* or however it was supposed to be pronounced Ed said "Larkin," just her name, and Larkin knew it meant *Larkin, pay attention*, she'd heard it enough times in her life to understand that particular translation, and she didn't have to hear it here. Not in some volunteer chorus for some Corrid*ork*estra in the middle of nowhere. She could leave— why had she never thought of that before?—and she did.

She left her score on her chair. Anni would know what to do with it. She took her purse, stood up, and walked off the stage. Ed didn't stop the choir. She could still hear them singing, all the way down the hall towards the stage door, which didn't open right away, Larkin had to lean into the panic bar a little harder than usual, and as soon as she got it open enough to see outside she saw why.

It was Harrison, collapsed on the steps, his body crumpled over itself.

That's where he'd been, all this time.

CHAPTER 4

When Larkin had finished giving both her statement and her fingerprints, she was escorted back into the police station lobby. Her mother was waiting for her, dressed in the same ratty sweatpants and college-logo hoodie that she must have been wearing when Larkin texted *you won't believe this but I found a dead body and I have to go to the police station.* Larkin hadn't been allowed to touch her phone after that; she assumed her mother must have replied with something that read as eminently reasonable and practical but actually meant *MY BABY! MOMMY'S COMING!* Her mother was so rarely like that—she had told Larkin, at one point, that to think of a child as "mine" in any sense beyond the relative was to ignore their unownable personhood—that whenever her mama-bird instincts overrode her more rational personality, Larkin assumed it was her job to comfort her mother and not the other way around.

So Larkin said, "It's okay, Mom, I'm fine," and the police officer who had led her back to the lobby echoed, "It's okay, Mom, she's fine." The officer, a woman with square shoulders and a blunt bob, smiled. "It's so rare that I get to tell parents that their kid isn't in trouble that I have to make the most of it." She held out her hand. "Claire Novak."

"Josephine Day," Larkin's mother said, standing and accepting Officer Novak's handshake. "What happened?"

"Well, your daughter called 911 after finding a man collapsed outside of the orchestra hall," Officer Novak said. "Of course, we had to show up and do some questioning, but Larkin here did really well and now y'all can go home."

"They took Ed, too," Larkin said. "Dr. Jackson." She had run back into the theater as soon as she saw Harrison's body, not stopping until she'd reached Ed's podium. She hadn't wanted to shout. She hadn't known what to say. She hadn't even been sure Harrison was dead, not until she and Ed were standing next to Harrison's body, waiting for the paramedics and the police to arrive. To fill the silence before the sirens—and to keep Ed from collapsing next to Harrison—she had kept them both talking, asking questions about where Ed lived and whether he liked teaching and then, when she had run out of everything else she could think of to ask, why he had chosen to conduct Beethoven's Ninth.

"I didn't choose it," Ed had told her. "They chose me for it. But I know the piece pretty well. I was one of the soloists in grad school."

He had said all of that as if he weren't listening to any of the words that were coming out of his mouth. Then he looked at Larkin as if he were seeing her for the first time. "You'll understand this," he said, "because you do theater. Music is all about tension and release. It's a cycle, just like the one you have in a story or in Shakespeare. Not everyone understands that. They think music is supposed to create some *feeling* inside of you, and they sit down in the concert hall ready to have that feeling—"

"In this case, joy—"

"Right! And then they daydream through the entire piece and get excited when it comes to the one part that they actually know."

Ed had always wanted to say this to someone; Larkin could tell. "You want to know how to really feel joy during Beethoven's Ninth Symphony?" he continued. *"Pay attention to the music.* Let yourself experience the cycles. It's all there, if you *listen.* I mean—"

The sound arrived before the lights; Larkin and Ed both flinched, then stood silently as vehicles and uniforms and stretchers appeared and disappeared. Then the police had separated the two of them, for questioning.

"Is he okay?"

"Yep, we let him go," Officer Novak said. "We've got all the information we need. Are you all good to get home?"

"My car's still at the theater," Larkin said.

"We can get your car tomorrow," her mother told her, putting a protective arm around Larkin's shoulders.

"I can drive!" Larkin said. "You can drop me off." She wanted her car. She wanted the past four hours not to have happened. She wanted Harrison to be alive again, not bent over with a swollen, purple face that the EMTs had understood immediately.

"I'd rather just get you home."

"You've got a good mom," Claire Novak said. "Let her take care of you."

"Oh, I already do," Josephine said. "She lives in my house." That was the kind of mothering Larkin recognized —brusque but comfortable, like being rubbed down with a fresh-from-the-dryer towel. She was about to return the affection, but in the second it took her to see if she could think of anything cleverer than *not on purpose*, Officer Novak spoke instead: "There you go. Keeps things simple."

"Well, tonight it does," Larkin's mother said. Her arm piloted Larkin's shoulders towards the door; then it paused. "Thank you for watching out for her."

"No problem," Officer Novak said—and then she nodded her head, just slightly, and Larkin watched her mother nod back. Except her mother didn't usually blush when she nodded, and she didn't usually smile when she was leading her daughter out of a police station, and as soon as they were in the car Larkin said, "Mom, do you have something you need to tell me?"

"I was about to ask the same thing," Josephine said. "What happened?"

Larkin had already told this story to Ed, the paramedics, and Officer Novak, so she tried to get through it as quickly as possible. "I was walking out the stage door and I saw Harrison, the accompanist, on the steps. His body was bent over and at first I thought he had just fallen down or something, but he didn't respond when I said his name, and his lips and his cheeks weren't the right color. They were blue, kind of. Purple, maybe. So I went back into the rehearsal hall to get Ed. He told me to call 911, and he told everyone else to go out the other door, and we went and stood by Harrison's body until the ambulance arrived. And then the cops showed up, and they took Ed and I—sorry, Ed and me—in for questioning."

She looked down at her hands. "I got fingerprinted, too. The woman who did it said I had more age lines on my left hand than my right hand. That doesn't make sense. Why would my non-dominant hand look older than my dominant one?"

"I have no idea," her mother said.

"I'm too young to have old hands," Larkin said. "It isn't fair. This whole evening has been terrible."

"I know, honey." The two of them sat quietly as Josephine took the Pratincola exit; they continued to sit quietly after Josephine pulled the car into her garage. "I'm sorry you had to go through all that."

"I don't want Harrison to be dead," Larkin said. The garage was filled with boxes of Christmas decorations and assorted detritus from Larkin's childhood. Her mother had gotten rid of a lot of it when she moved to Pratincola, but there was Larkin's old red tricycle with streamers hanging off the handles, right next to her mother's old ten-speed. They used to bike together, in Tacoma. Larkin felt like she might cry, and she really, really didn't want to.

"Can we make some hot cocoa?" she asked, even though it was too warm for cocoa and she didn't need to ask permission to get herself a snack. "And then could we make mug cakes, and put a hole in the mug cake, and pour the cocoa into the hole in the mug cake, and put a marshmallow in to plug up the hole in the mug cake, and then squirt so much whipped cream on the top that it falls over?"

"Sure," Larkin's mother said. Neither of them moved.

"I was afraid to call 911. I didn't want to cost Harrison a bunch of money. I thought he'd have to pay for the ambulance." The garage light shut off. Larkin kept talking. "Ed was the one who knew what to do. I was the one who saw a body and ran inside."

"You did fine," her mother said. "Claire Novak said you did really well."

"I didn't want to do any of it," Larkin said. "I'd never seen an ambulance before, that close. I'd never been inside a police station."

"Well, sometimes you just have to do the hard things. Especially when they're the right things."

They sat together, still. Larkin wondered if it was past midnight yet; if it had stopped being the day Harrison died and started being the day after. "Are you going to go to work tomorrow?"

"Yes." It was as if getting up would make the whole thing real, or over, or unbearably sad. Larkin had to say something, *anything*, about something else.

"Did you like that lady police officer?"

"What?" Josephine said, unbuckling her seatbelt and opening the car door—but in the moment before she exited the car, Larkin swore she saw her mother blush again.

CHAPTER 5

The funeral was small; Larkin, sitting in the very last pew, was one of maybe 30 people there. Thirty-three, she counted—because she had nothing else to do but *pay attention to the details*—including herself, the minister, and Anni at the piano. She had not approached the casket. Her memory already contained the image of Harrison at rest, though she hadn't realized what she was seeing when she first saw his face, eyes closed and jaw slack. She had assumed he had been hurt somehow, but she hadn't checked his breathing or his pulse or tried to remember the CPR training she took at the beginning of graduate school. Instead, in one of those character-revealing moments that never seem to reveal anything good, she'd run back into the orchestra hall to get Ed— who was currently sitting in the front pew, next to the woman who had just risen to give the eulogy.

"Of all the things you never think you're going to have to do," she said, "speaking at your ex-husband's funeral is so. . . insurmountably improbable that it doesn't even make the list."

Harrison's ex-wife was trim, tall, put together. Larkin wondered what had happened between them. The woman seemed like the kind of person who would be very interesting to know: sharp, clever, with a deep, warm laugh that set thirty-two members of the sanctuary at ease.

"Harrison and I had our differences, but I am honored to be able to speak to his life this afternoon." The program had indicated that Harrison was preceded in death by both his parents and an older brother; the woman standing at the lectern next to the casket must have been his closest ex-relation.

"If you knew Harrison at all, you knew that he'd only set foot in a church if he were getting paid—which, thanks to the way he decided to earn a living, meant he was there every Sunday. Wednesdays too, when he played for St. Pat's. Some years he'd play three Christmas Eve services back-to-back, because the Methodists liked to be done before dinner and the Presbyterians liked to start after dinner and the Catholics didn't even get rolling until midnight."

Laughter, again. Larkin had never been to a funeral before. She hadn't expected there to be jokes.

"So he knew his Bible, even though he thought the only part worth reading was the Song of Solomon. Which, in addition to some of its more risqué passages, reminds us that love is strong as death. Stronger than divorce, that's for sure." Now the woman was crying, putting down the paper she was holding and pulling a tissue from the little plastic packet that rested on the lectern. "Harrison loved so many things and so many people, so let's remember him by loving what we love and who we love." The woman had either not written an ending to her eulogy or had decided not to use it; either way, she was improvising. Badly. "And. . . let's have a moment of silence."

This meant that everyone in the sanctuary got to hear Harrison's ex-wife blow her nose into her tissue. Larkin saw a few heads drop, assumedly in prayer; she almost dropped hers as well (*kinesthetic response*) but kept it up to watch the pastor ascend the altar to comfort Harrison's ex-wife and then walk her back to her seat in the front pew. Anni, at the piano, was also alert; Larkin watched her watch the room and then carefully turn the page of her hymnal and begin a series of slow chords. Harrison had been dead even before Larkin had opened the stage door to find him, he had been dead when she and Ed had given statements to the police, and he had been dead when Ed sent the choir the news via email, but this felt like the beginning of his actual death; the moment when he passed from a person who was discussed as if he mattered to a person who would only be mentioned in recollection.

But they still had to finish the funeral, which meant they still had to stand and sing—Larkin heard Jessalyn's soprano soar to the stained-glass windows—and then pray again and then watch as the casket was carried out of the church. Ed was one of the pallbearers. So was Gerald. Larkin's position in the last row meant she was stuck waiting for the rest of the assembled to file out behind the casket, so she watched: the ex-wife, still sniffling into the same tissue; Jessalyn, who had accessorized her flowing black dress with a stunning black hat and walked out on the arm of a man Larkin didn't know; a very old woman attached to both a wheelchair and an oxygen tank, pushed by a younger woman wearing a black cardigan, rubber shoes, and a paper mask pinched around the bridge of her nose.

Then it was Larkin's turn to fall in and file out—but she turned the other direction. She hadn't wanted to say goodbye to Harrison's body, which had stopped being him the moment it collapsed on the cement steps. Now that the service was over and the body had been removed—borne, the opposite of born—she felt this compulsion to make some kind of gesture. Not like it would matter, not like Harrison could tell, but maybe he could. Maybe he could see her walk towards the altar and put her hand on the framed photograph next to the bouquet of flowers. Maybe that was for her, not for him. It wasn't as comforting as she thought it would be, but it was better than doing nothing.

"I'm sorry I didn't do more to help you," Larkin told the photograph.

Then Larkin noticed that the woman who had given the eulogy had left her notes behind, a piece of printer paper quartered by creases. Larkin picked it off the lectern, folded it back together again, and slipped it into her purse. She'd read it later, see what ending Harrison's ex-wife had written and then abandoned. She heard Anni turn a page and begin another hymn; her eyes followed the sound back to its source and saw that Anni, whose eyes were focused on her music, was smiling.

———

"How was the service?" Larkin's mother asked, when Larkin returned.

"It was fine," Larkin said. "Not a lot of people there."

"They might have had to work," Josephine said.

Larkin hadn't exactly forgotten what day it was, but she had forgotten what they meant. It was Thursday, exactly one week after Harrison's death, not yet noon. Her mother had taken a quick break from the college administrative office to have lunch and, apparently, grill her daughter about her life and friendships and grieving process.

"Were there a lot of people you knew?"

"Not a lot of people from the choir. Ed Jackson was there. A couple of the soloists. Also the woman who sits next to me at rehearsal. One of the altos."

"Oh, so you had someone to sit with. That's good."

"No, she was the pianist for the service." Larkin took the plate her mother offered her: a sandwich, turkey with tomato and lettuce and mayonnaise, and an orange cut into quarters. She began digging her finger into the edge of the orange peel. "I think she's going to get all the gigs Harrison used to play, and she seems thrilled about it."

"I suppose that's good for her," Josephine said. Larkin watched her mother watch her eat her orange. "How are you doing?"

"I'm fine," Larkin said, though she wasn't sure that was true. She wanted to tell her mother everything, and she also didn't want to tell her mother anything.

"Should I have gone with you?"

"No, it's cool," Larkin said. "I'm, like, an adult." She picked up her sandwich, looked at the soggy lettuce leaf poking out of one corner, and put it down. "It's just weird how we all go stand in a room to sum up someone's life and then we're supposed to, like, go back to whatever we were doing."

"And what part of your life are you going to get back to this afternoon?"

Larkin pulled the lettuce leaf out of her sandwich, tossing it into the side of the sink that had the garbage disposal. "Do I no longer get to play the *I found a dead body* card?" Larkin still hadn't told her mother that Harrison had asked her on a date, in part because he actually hadn't. Anyway, it didn't matter now. "I guess I'll work on the dissertation."

She saw what her mother did not say.

"I'm going to get it done, Mom. I swear."

But after Larkin's mother had gone back to the office and Larkin had gone into the guest bedroom, peeling off the little black dress that she had almost worn to the previous rehearsal and was *not* going to wear to that night's rehearsal—which was still on, the whole production was still going to happen, they were going to have to assemble on the Art Deco stage and sing about joy—she pulled on a T-shirt, got under the covers so she wouldn't have to wear pants, opened her laptop, and searched Harrison's name.

There was nothing here she hadn't already seen. News articles about various concerts and musicals that Harrison had accompanied. A handful of photos. One of them included the woman Larkin now recognized as his ex-wife, identified in the caption as Carla Ramirez. The ex-wife was on social media, none of it locked down, so Larkin scrolled past photos of Carla Ramirez Buckholtz's dogs and teenage stepchildren and human resources awards, a young son turning into a baby and then into a pregnancy and then the wedding photos, Dave Buckholtz, they seemed happy. That was as far back as her accounts went. Harrison hadn't created any social media profiles, of course. Larkin had guessed as much even before she started looking for them.

Then she opened the folder that contained the theoretical draft of her dissertation and all of its associated notes and ephemera. She had decided, back when the topic still sounded exciting, to analyze the way playwrights foreshadowed character death before and after Chekhov. To see if the infamous "Chekhov's gun" theory—a gun in the first act must go off in the second act—really changed anything, or if playwrights had been doing that kind of stuff since before Shakespeare. Larkin hadn't realized when she initially proposed the topic that Chekhov's theory wasn't just about guns. It was actually about the economy of details; the idea that anything a storyteller included in a story, or a playwright included in a play, or a director included in the staging of said play, had to be there for a reason. This was one of the reasons why Larkin's dissertation had slowed down.

But it was hard to focus on the dramatics of death—her tentative, working title—when she now knew someone who had actually died. Not that she hadn't known people who had died, but they had been great-grandparents, great-aunts, a high school football star who had been killed in a car accident when Larkin was in junior high. She hadn't cried for any of them. She still hadn't cried for Harrison.

So she searched his name again, this time adding phrases like "cause of death" and "how died," because that was the one piece of information that Larkin did not know. She had thought they'd mention it at the funeral, but it never came up. The obituary simply stated that Harrison Tucker, aged 53, "died unexpectedly," which the internet claimed was code for everything from heart attack to drug overdose.

Then Larkin remembered the eulogy, and scanned the guest bedroom floor for her little black purse, which she only ever wore with that little black dress and which was now partially hidden under the dress and its accompanying bra. She slid out of bed, undid the purse's little silver clasp, and pulled out the folded sheet of paper. Then she crouched on the carpet and read it.

Of all the things you never think you'll have to do, this
doesn't even make the list
Had our differences but honored to speak
Only set foot in church if getting paid
Three X-mas services
Knew his Bible, Song of Solomon
Love is strong as death (stronger than marriage)
Its jealousy unyielding as the grave
I used to wish he would die, not the only one
But now that we're here Solomon was wrong
Jealousy fades with time
Love lasts forever
Harrison loved many things many people
Let's remember that when we remember him
And remember to love

Carla had written her notes in black cursive, each line of words running slightly upwards. Her writing was even, orderly, with a slightly larger space before the word *die*, as if she had written *I used to wish he would* and then hesitated before committing to the truth. That was the part she had decided not to say, at the funeral. *I used to wish he would die. Not the only one.*

Larkin got back under her covers, her bare legs suddenly goose-prickled. Harrison's death had been unexpected. What if it had been planned? What if one of the people who wished he would die had made their wish come true?

It didn't make sense—like, someone murdering Harrison meant that they would have had to decide to kill him and *then do it*—but it was a thought that Larkin found difficult to ignore. Carla's abandoned eulogy. Anni's smile. Jessalyn's inability to sing in Harrison's presence. All of the tense looks that had gone around that circle of altos when Harrison's name was mentioned. Enough people disliked Harrison that his ex-wife had almost felt comfortable enough to joke about it at his own funeral.

But someone would still have had to decide to kill him, and then figure out how to kill him, and then do it. Not with a gun, or by strangling, or any of the physically obvious ways, because there'd been no sign of that—or at least the cops hadn't asked Larkin about it when she'd given her statement. She hadn't remembered blood; his face had been purple, but not bruised. He could have hit his head, maybe. Or been poisoned. Or suffocated.

Or not. Harrison could have just died, of anything from a heart attack to a drug overdose. It was so obviously *not murder* that Larkin told herself to stop fantasizing about solving it—and yet there she was, picturing herself telling Ed and everyone else on the orchestra hall stage that Harrison had been killed on purpose, and that she knew who did it. Uncovering Harrison's murderer was the most ridiculous idea Larkin had ever had, because there was *no way he'd actually been murdered*, but there had to be more to Harrison's death than what had been printed in the obituary.

If she could figure out what had actually happened in those last moments of Harrison's life—whether or not it was murder—maybe she could figure out what to do with the rest of hers.

CHAPTER 6

Rehearsal that evening was both short and subdued; Ed, whom Larkin assumed had followed Harrison's body all the way to the grave, still carried a sort of pall. He led them through what was usually Larkin's favorite type of rehearsal—a run-through without stops, followed by a few comments on what they did right rather than what they did wrong—and then dismissed them early.

"Sorry for all of you who drove out here just for that," he said. "It's been a long day. Most of you know that we buried Harrison this afternoon. I'm still processing everything that's happened over the past week, and I'm sorry I can't give you my better self tonight."

"It's okay," one of the front-row sopranos said. "Take some time. Take care of yourself."

"Thanks," Ed said. "I also wanted to thank you all for working so hard over these past few weeks. Your next rehearsal will be with the orchestra and our guest conductor Maestro Kimbrough, so you won't see me at the front of the room, but it's been a privilege. Thank you choir, thank you soloists, thank you Anni." Ben the baritone led a brief round of applause. "Now have a good night."

Larkin put away both her own chair and the chair Anni was no longer sitting in. Then she waited until the majority of the choir had cleared out. She wanted to talk to Ed, who was currently in the middle of some kind of choral receiving line, everyone wanting to thank him or bid him farewell or do whatever they needed to do before they could leave. Larkin wanted to ask Ed if he thought Harrison could have been murdered.

When she finally approached him, he was packing up his things: his score, his baton, his aluminum water bottle. He picked up an envelope that had been behind his score, against the conductor stand. "I forgot to give Anni her check," he said. "For playing the past two rehearsals."

"She's getting paid?" One more reason to add Anni to the suspect list—and Larkin could not believe that she was developing a *suspect list*, but there it was.

"Yeah, and now I have to ask the orchestra board what to do with the money we still owe Harrison," Ed said. "Does it go back into the budget, or does it go to his heirs? Does he even have heirs?" He put on his jacket. "I hope we don't have to get lawyers involved over a couple hundred bucks."

Larkin followed Ed as he went to turn off the stage lights. The darkened stage felt familiar and comfortable and sad, like an empty house that belonged to somebody else now. "Are you sorry that you won't get to direct the orchestra?"

"I never thought I would," Ed said. "I'm a voice guy." They continued down the hall towards the stage door. "I am sad I won't get to perform with you all, though."

"I'm sure they'd let you sing," Larkin said. "It's a volunteer choir, right? Just go stand with the basses or something."

"Except I'm a tenor," Ed said, smiling. Then he sighed. "Right now, all I want to do is go home. It's been a long day. A long week."

"For sure," Larkin said, as they continued down the hall towards the stage door. "I'd never given a statement to the police before."

Ed turned, glanced at her, didn't say anything. She wondered if he had. Then she wondered if wondering if he had was racist.

They exited the theater, walking down the steps where Harrison had died. They'd missed the sunset; the night was already dark, with moths fluttering at the streetlights. Larkin knew that the question she had wanted to ask would sound foolish, out here by the trash cans and the parked cars and the heavy, wet air. She couldn't tell Ed that she thought Harrison might have been murdered based on a half-sentence in an abandoned eulogy that she'd stolen from a church lectern. But that didn't mean she couldn't conduct her own investigation.

"I could give that check to Anni," Larkin said. "If you wanted to go home."

"Would you?" Ed said. "She actually lives near campus. Above the coffee shop."

"Which coffee shop?"

"You haven't been in Pratincola for very long, have you," Ed said. "There's only one."

"A town with only one coffee shop," Larkin said, taking the envelope from Ed, folding it in half, and sliding it into the back pocket of her jeans. "Impossible to imagine. You know I used to live in L.A."

"I know," Ed said. "So did I." Larkin hadn't expected

that. She wanted to ask Ed how he ended up in Iowa, though she assumed it was the usual way: a tenure-track position opening up at the right time and the wrong place. "We'll have to talk about it sometime," he continued. "But not tonight. Tonight I am going home and going to bed."

Which he did—and Larkin began the drive towards the place she did not yet consider home, to give Anni a check for $50 and figure out if she was one of the people who had wanted Harrison dead.

———

The glass doors to the apartment building were unlocked, which was the easy part. From there, Larkin found the mailroom and then Anni's apartment number. She had to look at the check to figure out Anni's last name, but there it was, *Morgan 532*, which meant it was time to take the elevator to the fifth floor. Except the elevator required a keycard, so Larkin had to hang around the lobby until someone came in, follow them onto the elevator, and then —no, they only wanted the fourth floor, so she got off on four, waited until they were far enough away that she could take the elevator back down to the lobby, and followed the next person who got on the elevator and, thankfully, pushed the 5. This would have been a lot easier if the building had buzzers, or if she knew Anni's phone number. It also wouldn't have been as much fun.

Because it was fun. Larkin approached 532 with a silly grin that she could not swallow. She was solving a mystery, just like the detectives on TV or the journalists on true-crime podcasts. She was standing outside of Anni Morgan's door, listening for suspicious noises—there was thumping going on in there, some definite thumping—and then knocking.

And then knocking again.

She hadn't expected Anni not to answer, so she kept at it, a continuous knock to drown out whatever murderous thumping noises were going on inside until the thumping stopped and the doorknob turned.

"Hey," Anni said. She was wearing black pajamas with not-quite-anatomically-correct skeleton bones printed on them. Her apartment was dimly lit and smelled like she'd been baking. Larkin was pretty sure the skelly jammies were enough to knock Anni off her suspect list, but she decided to continue with her investigation. For practice.

"I have a check for you," Larkin said. "From Ed." This was not good practice.

"Oh!" Anni said. "I wasn't expecting that. Not right away, anyway. Most of my clients pay on a net 30. I'm sorry, I should invite you inside. Would you like to come inside?"

Those were more words than Larkin had ever heard Anni speak in succession. She followed Anni into the apartment. It was a little hard to see everything, thanks to the fact that Anni appeared to be living by the light of an orange candle and her glow-in-the-dark pajamas, but it was impossible to miss the fact that Anni lived in a studio that was about half the size of a hotel room, and that her home included one twin bed; one small sofa with coffee table, one even smaller desk with laptop; one full-size digital piano, currently open, with a pair of earbuds resting on its keys; and something along the lines of forty-seven plants. More plants than Larkin could count, anyway. There were succulents and cacti and spider plants and a few deep-green leafy things that Larkin didn't know the names of, covering every available countertop and windowsill and most of the coffee table.

"Should I turn the lights on?" Anni said. "I like to keep it dark at night, for the melatonin."

"That's. . . fine," Larkin said. "I don't plan on staying long. Wouldn't want to mess up your melatonin production."

"I mean, I have melatonin tablets in the bathroom if it comes to it, but it's so much nicer if it's produced naturally, right?" Anni was bustling around the corner of her studio that served as a kitchen, taking down mugs and turning on an electric kettle. "Would you like a cup of tea? Or water? I don't have anything else, so it will have to be one of those. I do have seventeen different kinds of tea."

Anni's slippers had red and blue puffballs at the toes. There was a nerd cruise brochure sticky-tacked above her desk—a ship, a bunch of dice, a Kraken holding a keytar—next to what appeared to be a series of inspirational quotes, though it was too dark to read them. The smell Larkin had noticed earlier was definitely coming from the candle.

"Sure, I'll have a cup of tea," Larkin said, even though she didn't really want one. She should really hand Anni the check that was still folded in her back pocket and leave. "I don't care what kind. Whatever you're having."

"Well, I'm having poop tea," Anni said, "and I know not everybody wants that, so how about I give you cinnamon and spice instead?"

"Great," Larkin said. "It'll match the rest of the apartment."

Anni turned to Larkin and smiled. This smile was different from the one she used at the piano; it was a decision, not an impulse. "I never have visitors," she said. "I like it." She clicked off the kettle and poured two cups of tea. "Sit anywhere you like. Not on the bed."

Larkin sat on the sofa. Anni scootched forward on the piano bench. They were maybe three feet apart. They sipped their tea.

"Are you liking Pratincola?" Anni asked.

"I think Harrison was murdered," Larkin answered.

Anni reached backwards, took a coaster off the piano, and set it and then her tea on the floor. "Okay," she said. "Why, though?"

"Because—I don't know, his ex-wife left her eulogy at the church and she wrote something in it about how a bunch of people wanted him dead."

"You think that means somebody actually killed him?"

"Don't you think it's strange, how he died?"

"I don't know," Anni said. "I assumed it was a heart attack or an aneurysm or something. But then they never said, so I thought it might have been alcohol-related. He drank a lot."

"Yeah, I know. I saw him drinking during rehearsal."

"Wow," Anni said. "I didn't think it was that bad."

"He had a flask in his bag," Larkin said. "He told me not to tell anyone."

"Two can keep a secret if one of them is dead," Anni said. This time she smiled without thinking, and then thought better of it. "I'm sorry—can we make jokes? I think we have to. I'm going to say we can."

"I have the eulogy here," Larkin said. She had folded it up and zipped it into her wallet, for safekeeping; if she put it down among the boxes and stacks and piles in her mother's guest bedroom, there was no guarantee she'd find it again, or at least not without a search. Now she unzipped and unfolded and handed it to Anni, who crouched her glowing bones next to the coffee table and its cinnamon-scented candle so she could read it.

"We sang that piece, my first year in the choir," she said. "Love is strong as death, its jealousy unyielding as the grave." She looked up at Larkin, the light casting summer-camp-flashlight shadows under her eyes. "That might have been when Harrison was finalizing his divorce, I don't know. I've only ever known him not married. But we could look it up, if you think that's important."

"It could be," Larkin said. "But I don't think Carla did it."

"Who do you think did it, then?"

Something about the candle and the warmth of the tea and the absolute ridiculousness of Anni's skeleton pajamas spurred Larkin to honesty. "I almost thought it was you. You were my primary suspect. I didn't have a second one."

Anni, still on the floor next to her coffee table, began laughing so hard the candle flickered. "You thought I killed Harrison, and you came up here to—what, citizen's arrest?"

"Well, investigate first."

"Am I cleared?"

"Yes," Larkin said. "I can't imagine you killing anyone."

"Oh no, I used to kill my plants all the time," Anni said, scooting over to pick up her cup of tea and then settling herself on the sofa's other cushion. "But they were mercy killings. Only when the plant was mostly all the way dead." She sipped her tea. "Why did you think it was me?"

"Because you were the one who directly benefited from his death," Larkin said, not knowing if she should nudge herself closer to the armrest to give Anni more room.

There were maybe three inches between them now, instead of three feet. "And you seemed happy."

"I was happy that Dr. Ed asked me to play the Beethoven," Anni said. "And I'll probably get asked to play more gigs, now that Harrison isn't around. Which will be fun, but it's not worth murdering someone over. That stuff pays, like, $25 a rehearsal. Pretax."

"I know," Larkin said. "I peeked at the check."

"Wow, you really are the detective." Anni smiled, sipped her tea again. "Did you ask yourself how I would have done it?"

"No." Larkin hadn't gotten that far in her detecting.

"Well, I'll tell you, because it would have been very simple. I would have taken Harrison's epinephrine injector out of his bag, and then swapped whatever allergy-free cookie he picked up with one from the allergen table."

"Harrison has—"

"A life-threatening peanut allergy," Anni said, nodding. "Everyone knows that. I assumed you did too, since you were always eating off the allergy-free snack tables."

"I always picked the ones that had the shortest lines," Larkin said. Then she put it together. "Wait, is that what AF meant? I thought it meant—"

"No you did *not*," Anni said, laughing again. Her mug bounced, sloshed tea onto one pajama leg. "Fart-nuggets! Now I've spilled poop tea on my fake femur."

"Okay, wait." Larkin wasn't going to let herself get fooled again. "What is poop tea?"

"It's the tea that makes you go poop," Anni said. "The aloe does it. I have a licorice version too, but this tea's for both pooping and sleeping. I mean, you do the sleeping first." She tapped her wrist against the non-tea-splashed leg;

a watch face briefly lit up her corner of the sofa. "I should tell you that it's almost my bedtime—I mean, it obviously isn't, my heart rate is still way too high, it's always like that after I practice, and then you telling me about a *maybe murder* didn't help, but I'm going to do my meditation sequence and then write in my journal and then go to bed."

Larkin had no idea how to respond to this. Luckily, Anni did. "Which is why I'm kicking you out, in the very politest way. I've got work tomorrow, but I'll see what I can figure out about how Harrison died. You'd think if it had been anaphylactic shock they would have told us, but maybe not."

"I don't have work tomorrow," Larkin said, letting Anni take her mug and put it in the sink. "Maybe I could figure it out."

"Do you know how to find out how someone died?"

"No."

"Neither do I," Anni said. "So I'll start by searching *how to find out how someone died*." There was a small purple notebook on top of the piano; she wrote in it and held the paper up for Larkin to see. "There, I wrote it down so I'll remember to do it."

"I guess I'll just have to remember it without writing it down."

"No, you can have this one," Anni said, writing something else on the piece of paper, tearing it out of the notebook, and handing it to Larkin. "I'll write it down again. Also, I wrote down that we should meet tomorrow afternoon and discuss what we've learned. There's a coffee shop on the first floor of my apartment, which I'm assuming you already figured out, so let's meet there at 3 p.m., if that works for you."

All times worked for Larkin. "Sure," she said, taking

Anni's paper, folding it in half, and putting it into her—
"Wait, I almost forgot, I still have your check."

"Excellent," Anni said, taking it and walking Larkin to the door. "Thank you for bringing it, and thank you for deciding that I wasn't a murderer."

"I could still change my mind," Larkin said.

"I'll see you tomorrow," Anni told her.

CHAPTER 7

The next morning Larkin's mother asked her the usual question—"what are your plans for today?" —and, two days running, Larkin had an answer. Half an answer, anyway.

"I'm going to meet up with someone from the choir."

"Oh, you've made a friend!" Josephine only looked a little delighted. Larkin suspected her mother was holding back. "Anyone I know?"

"Anni Morgan. She was the pianist at the funeral yesterday. We're going to get coffee this afternoon." Larkin didn't mention that they were also going to find out how Harrison died. She had decided that it was okay to keep at least some part of her life private, especially the part where she and the local accompanist figured out whether the other local accompanist had been murdered. Boundaries were important, after all.

"Well, I hope you have a lovely time," Josephine said. "I told you joining that choir was—"

"Don't say it."

"Fine," her mother said, trying not to smile. "But feel

free to bring your friends by the house any time you want. I can even stock up with snacks!"

"Mom." Larkin still knew how to pull off a perfect eyeroll. "You're not going to buy snacks for us." Then she twitched her nose to let her mom know she was only teasing. "I can order them myself online."

"Fifty dollars worth," Josephine said, twitching her nose in return. It had been their thing, back when Larkin was young. It seemed to have become their thing again. "Use my account, until you get a job of your own."

That deadened the moment—though Larkin didn't let her mom know—and most of the moments between when Josephine left for work and when it was time to meet Anni for coffee. Larkin spent a good hour catching up on news sites and social media feeds, then another hour reading about how dismal the academic job market was, then inadvertently put her face near her right armpit while reaching for the box of herb-and-mozzarella flavored crackers in her mom's cupboard and realized it was time to take a shower.

But she ate the crackers first, with some actual mozzarella (for the nutrition) and a handful of gummy dinosaurs (for *because she liked them*) that quickly became the entire bag, so she ordered another bag of gummies and another box of crackers and a thing of wasabi peas and a family-sized tub of malted milk balls and then the same family-sized tub but it was cheese balls this time, and that wasn't quite $50 so she threw in some dark chocolate because she knew her mom liked it, and then she got up from the sofa and swept the crumbs either into her hand or onto the floor, depending on various laws of physics that she didn't really understand.

Then she took a shower.

Then Larkin told herself she would work on her dissertation, because that was the first step in getting her life

Back On Track, but the real first step was cueing up the right dissertation-writing music and the second step was clicking on the ad that appeared next to the album, because maybe her life really would be better with a new kind of charcoal face mask. She hadn't bought one in forever, not since she maxed out one of her credit cards, but she'd made a payment on that card, so there was still money left for her to use if she wanted it.

No, she wouldn't. She'd bookmark the mask, though, in case she wanted to buy it later. It was actually a subscription service, so she'd need to pay every month—but then she'd get four masks per month, which was almost one per week, and it would come out to around $1.50 per mask with the coupon code, and that was a good deal.

But still no.

But she should clean out her bookmarks, while she was here.

Huh, she'd forgotten how funny that video was. She'd keep that one bookmarked.

Oh, there was that source she wanted to use in her dissertation. Time to get back to that project. She had—well, ninety minutes was better than nothing. She could get another thousand words into her draft, if she stayed focused.

Two hundred sixty-three words later, it was time to put on pants and meet Anni at the coffee shop.

Larkin was ten minutes late. Anni, wearing the same not-linen, not-leggings, not-sneakers she always wore with the addition of a nubbly gray cardigan, had claimed a table by the window. Her laptop was open; there was a utilitarian canvas satchel hanging off the back of her chair.

"Hi!" Anni said. "I ordered already, I hope you don't

mind. They have a really excellent house-made ginger tea, if you like that kind of thing."

Larkin ordered a double shot mocha with whip and charged it to the card that she hadn't used to buy the face mask. Then she joined Anni at the table.

"All right," Anni said. "I'm going to assume we did the same research."

"Sure," Larkin said. She had searched *how to find out how someone died*, but had only turned up a bunch of message boards full of people with the same question.

"So we're going to need to get the death certificate, which means we're going to need to find either a family member or a lawyer." Anni must have actually read the message boards.

"Harrison doesn't have a lot of family members," Larkin said. "At least as far as I could tell. His obituary said he was preceded in death by his parents and brother, and didn't mention him being survived by anyone."

"Right," Anni said. "And I don't think we need to go bother his grandmother about this." That was, presumably, the woman at the funeral with the wheelchair and the oxygen tank. "So we'll have to get to his lawyer, who can request the certificate for us."

"Did Harrison have a lawyer?"

"Well, he got divorced, so he must have at some point." Anni sipped her house-made ginger-flavored water. "Plus, now that he's dead, there's got to be someone dealing with his estate, though that doesn't necessarily have to be a lawyer. Just an executor." Larkin watched Anni think. It was like watching a dog's paws twitch while it dreamed. "Do you think Harrison made a will? He doesn't have any children that I know of, and he doesn't have that much money—that I know of. But he could have. I did an online will last year, it's very easy."

"Harrison didn't have a smartphone," Larkin said. "If he did his will himself, he wouldn't have done it online. He would have done it on paper."

"Probably on some dot matrix printer," Anni said. "Or a typewriter." She looked at Larkin. "We're still okay with jokes, right?"

"Joke away," Larkin said.

"Excellent." Anni smiled. "So we don't know who his lawyer is, but we do know who his CPA is, because I recommended her to him and then she thanked me for bringing her a new client."

"You have a CPA?"

"Of course," Anni said. "I'm a small-business owner."

"You own a business?" Larkin knew it wasn't a good idea to spout incredulous questions at a person whom she had recently decided wasn't a murderer and hadn't yet decided was a friend, but she couldn't help it.

"Technically a sole proprietorship," Anni said. "I write copy for financial services companies, software-as-a-service companies, that kind of thing. That's how I know about wills. I did this whole series of posts for a will-and-trust company, explaining how to create a valid will in each state. It was a fifty-post gig, and I got it done in two weeks."

"Okay, wait." One more question, and then they could get back to the investigation. "I thought you were a musician."

"I am a musician," Anni said.

"No, like—" Larkin looked at the bits of whipped cream clinging to the edge of her cardboard coffee cup. "I thought that's what you wanted to be. As your job." She swiped around the inner rim of the cup with her finger. "Do you know why I'm here?"

"Because we're trying to figure out how Harrison died."

"No, why I'm *here* here." Larkin put her whipped-cream-covered finger in her mouth before she remembered it was bad table manners. "In Pratincola."

"No," Anni said, pushing a square paper napkin in Larkin's direction.

"So. . ." Larkin wiped her hands and thought about how to begin. "I've wanted to work in the theater since I was, like, five years old. My mom—do you know who my mom is? Josephine Day. She's a dean now, but she was a professor when I was growing up, and I remember her taking me to this university production of *Camelot*, which I know I was way too young for, but I got it. Enough of it. And I loved it. And then she took me backstage, and I realized that all these people had *made* it. That grownups got to play with costumes and tell stories, just like I did with my dress-up box and my stuffed animals, and it was a real thing you could do for the rest of your life."

She looked at Anni, who was listening carefully, head cocked to one side, hands folded around the glazed clay mug that she must have known to ask for. "So I became your classic theater kid, school plays, summer camps, jazz hands from here to eternity, exactly what you'd expect. Except I knew I didn't want to do the starving actor thing, because I was already this tall and this wide and there was no market for that, and also because I grew up as an academic brat so I knew about the advantages of a tenure-track job. Decent pay, summers off, sabbaticals, job security. A pretty good deal."

Anni nodded. Larkin continued. "This meant I needed to get on the academic track, so I got my MA, did this stint in New York so I'd have some practical experience, came back to Los Angeles to do the PhD, started my disserta-tion, and. . ."

She'd come to the part of the story that she hated telling. That she'd never actually told anyone, not exactly. So she didn't tell it *exactly* to Anni, either—just that she'd stalled on her dissertation, tried the job market as a newly minted ABD ("that's All But Dissertation"), spent the next year hacking at the dissertation while simultaneously working as a rideshare driver and temping, both of which convinced her that the only job worth having was an academic job while simultaneously sapping her of all the energy required to finish her dissertation and go after said job. Then it was job market season again ("it's like you're a debutante, and they'd never cast me as the debu-tante") and then Larkin decided to take some time off ("it was just supposed to be two weeks, right?") and then it was time to pack up her corner of the apartment that she'd shared with two graduate students and three aspiring actors, and move to Iowa to live with her mother.

"So here I am, in the middle of nowhere, with a life full of crushed dreams," Larkin said, which was generally how she ended this story. Sometimes with an accompanying dramatic hand gesture, but her hands were busy turning her cardboard coffee cup into a cardboard coffee wad. Anni handed her a few more square napkins.

"I'm sorry about your dreams," Anni said. "But you aren't exactly in the middle of nowhere. Eastern Iowa is one of the best regions of the country to live in right now, whether you're calculating by affordability or opportunity. Cedar Rapids has a growing startup incubator, Iowa City has the top creative writing program in probably the entire world, we're one of the healthiest metro areas according to two independent ratings systems, and the Pratincola Cycle

Club just raised enough money to add protected bike lanes to the streets most often traveled by cyclists."

"So why are you here?" Larkin shoved the wet napkins into the folds of her crumpled cup. "You're talented. Why write about insurance or whatever when you could go be a musician?"

"I am a musician," Anni said again. "I don't think I understand your question."

"Like. . . *full-time.* As your career."

"But I like my career." Anni took another sip from her mug. "Oh, it's gone cold now." She put it down and took out her phone. "I shouldn't stay too much longer, since I'll probably have some emails I need to answer before the end of the day, and most of my clients are on Eastern time." She swiped and tapped and put her phone to her ear. "I'm calling my CPA to see if we can find out who Harrison's lawyer was. Or is, I'm not sure which applies."

Larkin watched as Anni conducted one side of an efficient conversation. "Hello, this is Anni Morgan. I'm well, how are you? Oh, what are you all dressing up as for Halloween? I bet you'll look great. I'll watch for the photos. No, my accounts are fine. Yes, still on target. I'm estimating just above six figures, if all of the checks come in on time. Yes, it's been an excellent year. I'm sorry, I'm actually calling because I had a question. About Harrison—yes, it was surprising. I went to the funeral. That's actually why I'm calling. I know you probably can't say, but I was curious if you knew who Harrison was using as his lawyer. Oh, of course. I understand. I appreciate your discretion. Well, thank you, and I hope you have a good weekend. Yes, much cooler! Perfect football weather. All right, you have a great rest of your day now."

Anni put her phone face-down on the table and shrugged. "She couldn't tell us. Accountant-client privilege. That's probably going to apply to the lawyer as well. Attorney-client privilege, not accountant-client privilege. This may be a dead end." She paused. "Pun intended."

"You barely asked, though," Larkin said. "You've got to go after your objective. Win the scene. We should have met her in person, instead of over the phone. Then I could have staged the conversation to manipulate her emotions—"

"That seems unfair—"

"Everything's fair until one character gets what they want. That's how theater works."

"I'm not sure I want to manipulate anybody," Anni said. "That doesn't seem right."

"You know what isn't right? Murdering somebody." Now Larkin was going after her objective in full. She leaned forward, forearms on the table, staring Anni down.

"We could just do some more internet research. Maybe I should look up *how to find the lawyer of someone who is dead*."

"You do that," Larkin said. She leaned back, ready to win the scene. "I'm going to have an in-person conversation with Carla Ramirez Buckholtz. First person to get the name of the lawyer wins."

"Fine," Anni said. "I mean, it doesn't have to be a competition." Larkin might have thought Anni meant it, except she had already picked up and unlocked her phone.

"Of course it does," Larkin said. "That's what's called raising the stakes."

———

"Larkin, how do you make an event?"

Larkin was, at that very moment, cutting up leftover braised steak to make stovetop quesadillas; she turned around to see her mother staring, as usual, at her laptop. "You mean, like, online?"

"Yes," Josephine said. "I want to throw a little gathering for people, now that we've gotten back into the swing of the semester. I've got the list here—" she gestured to a handful of names written on a yellow legal pad "—but I can't figure out how to do the thing."

Be specific, Larkin wanted to say. Her mother had spent years telling her to choose the right words and look up the ones she didn't know in the dictionary. To *figure it out yourself,* instead of asking an adult to give her the answer. That was when Larkin's mother had known everything about how the world worked. Now she, like every other parent, needed their children to show them how to create an event on social media.

Larkin added the chopped steak to a pair of tortillas that she had already started warming on the grill, then added a generous helping of grated cheese to each. Another pre-warmed tortilla went on top, and then she flipped them, pressing the rubber spatula down on each quesadilla to get the cheese and steak good and smashed. They used to make quesadillas with brick cheese, the cheap orange cheddar that came with the store's name on it instead of a cartoon image of a smiling cow. Larkin's mother would flip the quesadillas, trying to get the center of each cheddar slice to melt before the soft flour tortillas started to burn, and try to keep Larkin focused on her homework.

"What do *you* think you should do next?" Larkin asked, echoing the memory of her mother's words.

"Get my daughter, who lives rent-free in my house, to help me."

"Okay, fine. Let me finish making dinner." Larkin transferred the first quesadilla to a plate and set it in front of her mother, along with a jar of salsa, a tub of sour cream, and a soup bowl filled with Larkin's homemade guacamole (secret ingredient: brown sugar). They used to eat their quesadillas vegetarian, with ketchup, the two of them in a much smaller kitchen in Tacoma. Mom would keep the public radio station going all evening long, as she cooked and did the dishes and settled down to start grading papers. They never threw parties, then. The apartment wasn't large enough.

"So what are we hosting?" Larkin asked, once she sat down with her own plate of tortillas and melted cheese.

"Just a small gathering, happy fall, that kind of thing."

"Can it be a Halloween party?"

"No," Josephine said. "It's too early for that." She pushed her laptop in Larkin's direction. "Here."

Larkin took her mother's dictation, creating "A little get-together to celebrate fall" and setting the date for the upcoming Friday. "Mom, you can't make an event that's only a week away."

"Why not?"

"Because people get booked up, you know? They can't just drop everything to go to some get-together."

"Sure they can," Josephine said. "You don't have any plans for next Friday, right?"

"I'm starting to have more plans now," Larkin said. "So I could. You don't know."

"Well, you can invite anyone you like," Larkin's mother said, as if she did in fact already know. "Any of your new friends."

"Okay," Larkin said. She wasn't sure if Anni was a friend yet, but she was pretty sure that she didn't want to invite her to stand in the background of her mother's party.

"And make sure you invite everyone on that list," her mother continued.

"Sure you don't want to learn how to do this yourself?"

"I'm giving you something useful to do," her mother said, cutting the corner off her quesadilla and twirling the trailing cheese onto her fork. "Oh, I should also mention— I got you an interview."

Larkin stopped typing. "What kind of interview?"

"One of our administrative assistants is going on maternity leave," her mother said, between bites and swallows. "We're looking for someone to fill in for twelve weeks, and I thought you might be the perfect candidate."

"Isn't that nepotism?"

"Probably," her mother said, tearing off the next bite of quesadilla with her fingers. "But it's only for twelve weeks, and I won't be involved in the hiring process." She chewed and swallowed again. "The interview's Tuesday. Can you get me a paper towel?"

Larkin stood up, tore a towel off the roll by the sink, and handed both it and her disapproval to her mother.

"You need a job," her mother said.

"It's going to get in the way of my work," Larkin said back. She watched her mother decide not to comment; it didn't matter, of course, because the unsaid words filled the kitchen, clouding Larkin's eyes like steam. She sat down and continued adding guests to her mother's party, wiping the back of her hand across her cheek, picking up her quesadilla and biting into one end and immediately dribbling hot cheese grease down her wrist.

"Are you okay?" Josephine asked.

"I burned myself," Larkin said, even though she hadn't. It was an excuse, and that was what she needed at the moment—not a job, not the opportunity to invite new friends to spend time in her mother's backyard, not these tiny but incessant steps towards a life she didn't want in a place she didn't want to live.

She stood up again, ran cold water over her wrist, splashed herself on purpose. It didn't work.

"I know this isn't what you want," her mother said, as if Larkin's thoughts had also expanded beyond her body. "But it'll be good for you. It'll give you something to do while you figure out what you want to do next."

"I already have something to do," Larkin said, passing her mother's laptop back to her side of the table and pulling out her phone. She tapped at her own social media apps; accepted the invite that she had just sent herself. Then she began thumbing out an invite of her own, to Carla Ramirez Buckholtz.

"Hey," Josephine said. Larkin looked up; watched her mother twitch her nose. "It's going to be okay."

"Okay," Larkin repeated, looking back at her phone. There was a green dot next to Carla's profile pic; three dots at the bottom of the screen.

"Okay?" her mother said, a hint of anxiety in her voice.

"Okay," Larkin said again, twitching her nose back at her mother this time. It looked like it would be okay—the part of the story that was happening on her phone, the part she was making happen herself, not the part where she had to interview for some admin job to make her mother happy.

But that part wasn't until Tuesday.

Her interview with Carla would take place tomorrow morning.

CHAPTER 8

"You look lovely today," Josephine said.

"I'm your darling daughter," Larkin said. "You're supposed to tell me I look lovely every day."

"Well, you look exceptionally lovely today," Josephine said. Larkin had achieved this compliment by dressing exactly like her mother. She wore a nicer pair of jeans paired with one of the loose floral blouses she'd worn to her many unsuccessful job interviews—she wondered if it had bad juju, and then decided that, as a white woman who didn't even know where juju originated, she couldn't claim it applied to her blouse—paired with a cornflower-blue cardigan that her mother had thrust upon her two Christmases ago. Josephine, standing between the coffee maker and the toaster and waiting for their respective dripping and popping, was wearing the same cardigan in a slightly darker shade.

"You're also supposed to tell me that the beauty standard doesn't matter." Larkin had even dressed her hair like her mother's, after trying and failing to remember how to braid. Dean Day wore her just-below-shoulder-length dark hair with a single barrette in the back, keeping the strands that might have fallen in her face at bay; Larkin wore her should-have-gotten-it-trimmed-two-months-ago hair, in its matching shade, with a barrette that she had swiped from her mother's shelf in the bathroom. She had positioned herself in the kitchen so her mom couldn't see the back of her head.

"But beauty is truth," Josephine said. "And truth beauty. That's the standard, and it does matter." She put a slice of toast on a saucer and handed it to Larkin, along with a knife for the plastic butter tub that currently sat across from Josephine's laptop on the kitchen table.

"Are you sure Keats didn't mistranslate the words he found on that urn?"

"Larkin." Her mother laughed so hard she slopped coffee over the side of her mug. "Do you actually think that *beauty is truth, truth beauty* was written *on the urn?*"

"It's in the title of the poem," Larkin said, twitching her nose at her mom. "He finds an ode on a Grecian urn."

"I cannot believe I gave birth to you."

"So glad you did, though." Larkin finished her toast, scootched past her mother to wash the butter off her hands, quickly explained that she was meeting another friend for coffee and would be back before lunch— Josephine was thrilled that her daughter had made a *second friend*, never mind that this "friend" was really "a woman Larkin planned to interrogate about the death of her ex-husband in order to solve a murder and/or win a contest"—and was out of the house in just enough time to justifiably pretend she hadn't heard her mother say "are you wearing my barrette?"

———

Larkin met Carla at the coffee shop in Anni's apartment. This time, Larkin arrived early so she could get her seasonally appropriate pumpkin spice latte in a for-here mug and claim the perfect table. The two-top against the wall, downstage left, putting Carla in the corner of the room with her back to the window. Vulnerable, with no escape routes. Perfect for collecting information.

Of course, once Carla actually arrived, fresh and slightly sweaty from her Saturday morning HIIT class, she did not fall neatly into the role of the interrogatee. Instead, she adjusted her chair so that she could see out the window, cracked the top on her bottle of sparkling water, and said "You know you're not the first person to message me and ask to talk about Harrison."

"I'm not?" Larkin asked.

"No." Carla was not unfriendly about it. "You know I used to think it would stop after we divorced, and yet I'm still having these conversations after his death. I'm sorry. You must be grieving."

Director Larkin told Actor Larkin to make a choice. "Yes, I mean, it was so unexpected." That was a *yes*. She needed the *and*. "And finding him like that."

"You were the one who found him? I really am sorry." Carla sighed. "So you must be part of the orchestra thing. I told him to stop messing around with the people he worked with. Someone was going to file a complaint at some point. Now I suppose it doesn't matter."

"We weren't messing around," Larkin said. She wanted to stay as close as she could to the truth, while collecting as many additional truths as possible. "We were. . . I thought it might be love."

"Right," Carla said. "Of course you did. Again, I am sorry. I must seem very cold and callous."

"No, I saw you cry at the funeral." Larkin needed to

put Carla at ease. "You loved him too." *Yes.* "But you were mad at him." *And.*

"Well, I had to organize a funeral for a man who spent half a decade disrespecting the sacred bonds of marriage," Carla said. "He didn't even get the *death do us part* one right."

"So he cheated on you." Sometimes you just had to say the subtext out loud.

"I used to get emails from people," Carla said, "wanting to confess. Or commiserate, because he cheated on them, too. Harrison kept telling me that his love was too big to be contained, the heart wants what it wants, the usual stuff. Honestly, if he'd approached the subject the way people talk about it now, the whole ethical non-monogamy thing, I might have considered it."

Larkin could understand that. Carla and Harrison must have been a well-matched and intriguing pair. She could feel the same combination of energy, arrogance, and anger coming from Carla that she had felt during her few conversations with Harrison. Plus, Carla was devastatingly attractive, in that "older woman who could either take care of you or judo flip you to the ground" kind of way. She was wearing a pink tank top under her hoodie, and Larkin could see the hint of a well-toned shoulder.

"Is that why the two of you broke up?" Larkin stuck to her character—heartbroken innocent—and avoided using the word *divorced*.

"That's how all of Harrison's relationships ended," Carla said. "Even before we were married. He was in the middle of this long-term thing with this other woman, she was pushing him to get engaged, and then he met me. Let me give you a piece of advice: if someone cheats *with* you, they'll cheat *on* you."

Larkin had heard that aphorism before; it tended to

come up regularly in advice columns and talk shows. She had watched a lot of talk shows instead of writing her dissertation, and read a lot of advice columns. Her initial instinct was to explain all of this to Carla, to start in on the story of her Crushed Dreams, she had almost opened her mouth to begin, and then she realized that would be way, way out of character. So she froze.

Make a choice, Larkin told herself.

And then Carla made one.

"I don't believe the rumors, though. About that girl. If that's what you wanted to ask about."

This was now the only thing Larkin wanted to ask about. "I heard about that," she said, even though she hadn't.

"Look, I believe women," Carla said. "If that girl says someone put something in her drink, I'm sure it happened. But I don't think it was Harrison who did it. He liked to cheat at some parts of the game, but not that one. They all went willingly, and then they all came and told me about it afterwards." Her manicured nails tore at the label on her water bottle. "I mean, I guess he could have. But that would have made him a different person. Someone I didn't know at all."

"I'm sorry," Larkin said. Honestly. "It sounds like you really loved him."

"I've decided to remember him fondly," Carla said. "Probably what you should do, too." She stood up. "And now I've got to go. We're doing the pumpkin patch this afternoon. Take care of yourself, okay?"

She stood up, pulled her gym bag off the back of the chair, and was gone.

Larkin sat very, very still. She had not considered that somebody wanting Harrison dead could mean Harrison having done something terrible enough to justify his own death. Not that drugging a young woman meant you deserved to be murdered—if Harrison had actually done that, and Carla didn't believe he had. But. Still. Larkin wasn't sure she wanted to do this anymore. She had thought it would be a simple case of professional jealousy or something, which, like, did she even think about it? That kind of thing only happened in books, or the kinds of plays that were set in British country houses with an overabundance of doors.

This was real. Harrison had really died—and before that, maybe he put something in someone's drink.

Then Larkin's phone buzzed, and she pulled it out of the pocket of her cardigan. A text—no, a series of texts— from Anni.

Got the lawyer

Larkin had forgotten about the lawyer.

I did a search on my email for "harrison lawyer" and found some choir board meeting minutes from a year ago

Board minutes are public, sent to everyone in the choir

In which the board resolved to use the lawyer Harrison recommended

It was for an unrelated thing

Sam Nagel

Still don't think this is going to work though

Larkin held her phone and asked herself whether she wanted to continue with this investigation. Whether she wanted to tell Anni what she had learned from Carla. Whether it was better to stop now and remember Harrison fondly, or whether she had an obligation to uncover the truth about everything that had happened, whatever it turned out to be.

She texted Anni.

Am below your apt right now in coffee shop

Can we talk

It took a few minutes for Anni to arrive and a few seconds for Larkin to tell her. She sat in the chair Carla had vacated, turning it away from the window and towards Larkin. Her hands were clasped on the table; her voice was calm.

"So we have two mysteries to solve, then. Maybe three."

"Three?"

"One. Was Harrison murdered? Two—no, wait, I need to write this down."

Anni took her purple notebook and matching inkpen out of her utilitarian bag and began making an outline.

Q1: Was Harrison murdered?
*   If NO, then END INVESTIGATION*
*   If YES, then Q1.1 or TELL POLICE*

Q1.1: Can we figure out who did it?
*   If NO, then TELL POLICE*
*   If YES, then ALSO TELL POLICE*

Q2: Did Harrison drug a young woman (and/or more than one)?
*   If NO, then END INVESTIGATION*
*   If YES, then Q2.1 or SUGGEST WOMEN INVOLVED*
TELL POLICE?

Q2.1: Are these events related?

She turned her notebook so Larkin could read it. "What do you think?"

"Sure," Larkin said. "If we're going to do this, that seems like the way to do it."

"We could just go *here* right now," Anni said, tapping the part of the paper that read "TELL POLICE."

Larkin shook her head. "I already talked to them. When I found Harrison's body. We don't have any new information to tell them yet."

"All right, then." Anni closed her notebook and put it in her bag. "We can't work on Question 1 until next week, because lawyers don't work weekends. But we can start work on Question 2 right now, because nurses do."

"Are we just going to go ask a nurse—" Larkin didn't know exactly how HIPAA worked, but she was pretty sure that the rules for lawyers and CPAs also applied to medical professionals. Anni didn't answer; she had already put her phone up to her ear.

"Hi, this is Anni Morgan. They're doing fine, thanks for asking. She's doing fine too. Well, no, I hope she doesn't have to bring them back either! I was just curious if Nate was on shift today. Is he super busy? I have some questions for this project I'm working on, and—sure, put him on. Hey, Nate!"

Larkin watched Anni conduct a second efficient conversation. "Nate will talk with us," she said, after she'd finished the call. "Want to bike over to the medical center?"

CHAPTER 9

They ended up taking Larkin's car, because even though Larkin's phone claimed it was 69 degrees out, it also claimed the air was 81 percent humid —which was not a number Larkin had really paid attention to before moving to Iowa, but seemed to make all the difference in whether she wanted to spend any more time outdoors than she had to.

She still wasn't sure she wanted to spend any more time doing this, either, but Anni had said "it's only one meeting" and then "it's only four miles on the bike trail," and they'd compromised on the part where they were driving, not biking. When the parking garage turned out to be two blocks away from the part of the medical complex where they were meeting Nate, Larkin let the sweat gather on her upper lip and didn't say anything.

Anni had also gotten uncharacteristically quiet as they approached the pavilion that contained the cafeteria that contained their meeting—Larkin swiped her credit card, knowing this would probably be the last coffee she could buy on that card and not knowing how she'd pay the bill at the end of the month—though Larkin saw Anni give a cheerful boilerplate wave as soon as the man whom she assumed was Nate the nurse entered the room.

Nate was broad and blonde and genuinely pleased to see them, which Larkin immediately understood meant he was pleased to see Anni. He couldn't stop looking at her, glancing over his shoulder as he stood in line with a protein smoothie in one hand and a bottle of soda in the other. There were four seats at their table; Larkin had, without thinking, taken the one next to Anni. She got up and switched to one of the two opposite seats while Nate was paying.

"What are you doing?" Anni whispered.

"He wants to sit next to you," Larkin whispered back.

"Oh," Anni said. She looked a little disconcerted, but returned to her cheerful demeanor as soon as Nate approached their table. Then she scooted her chair over a few inches towards Larkin, to make room.

"Hey, Anni," Nate said. He noted Larkin's presence, nodded, and turned his attention back where it belonged. "How's your family doing?"

They talked for a few minutes about Anni's sister, who had twin boys and had last visited the emergency room for something related to "a treehouse farting contest." That was Nate's department: taking temperatures and teaching eight-year-old boys how to keep their stitches clean. They also talked about Anni's mother, who had—as Larkin gathered—recently completed chemotherapy and radiation. Not so recently that it was still a going concern, but recently enough that it was still an ongoing conversation.

"She was lucky," she heard Nate say, even though that wasn't his department. He appeared eager to reassure Anni that everything would be all right, from her nephews' latest injuries to her mother's three-month checkup. Anni was equally eager to dispense with the reassuring.

"Mom's doing what she's supposed to do," Anni said, "with the exercises and everything, and beyond that we're all just going to enjoy life."

"That's all you can do," Nate said.

"Right," Anni said. "Well, I'm glad you were able to meet up with us. I hope it doesn't turn out to be a waste of your time."

"It never is," Nate said. Larkin watched him figure out where to place his tension. He chose his shoulders.

"Right," Anni said again. Her tension was collecting in the space between her eyebrows. "Well, you don't have to answer if you don't feel comfortable, but we have a couple of technical questions about—"

"We're writing a musical," Larkin interrupted. She did not know exactly how Anni was planning to conduct this investigation, but she could tell that it would not go the way they wanted. Not with everything going on between Anni and Nate, and definitely not with whatever was going on between Anni and the inside of her head. "A murder mystery musical."

"That sounds like fun!" Nate was pleased. Anni less so.

"And we wanted to make sure we got all of the details right, you know?" Larkin was improvising, freewheeling, working on instinct. "Also, I'm new in town, and I wanted to make sure we didn't accidentally write something that was too close to the truth. You know, so people wouldn't think it was about them."

Nate nodded. Anni glared.

"So we wanted to ask you about roofies." Larkin stopped talking and waited for Nate to start. People are compelled to fill silences, and she was ready to see what

Nate filled this one with—and hoping that Anni wouldn't fill it instead.

"Rohypnol," Nate began. Anni was about to speak, Larkin saw the slightest intake of breath, and she kicked Anni hard under the table. "Well, you've got to make sure that it turns the glass blue. You could probably do that with food coloring. They changed the formula of the pills so that people would know if their drink had been tampered with."

He paused. Larkin waited. She knew he would speak again.

"They'd need to get the pills from somewhere, too. Unless you're setting your musical overseas. They don't sell Rohypnol in the U.S., but other countries still sell it as a sleeping pill."

"Does that mean you don't see a lot of people who have been roofied?" Larkin nudged the conversation in the direction she wanted it to go. "Like, how many cases do you get a year?"

Nate stared at the table. Whatever he had been worried about traveled from his shoulders to his hands, and he began passing his unopened soda bottle back and forth between them. "Well. . . um. . . a lot of women don't report, you know?"

"Sure," Larkin said. "There was this one time that I got drunk—way drunk, it was this party and they were serving cocktails that were pure alcohol—and the next day I didn't know what to do, and then I decided not to do anything." That was mostly true. "I mean, I thought I had food poisoning, because I was in my boyfriend's apartment and I couldn't stop throwing up. I got blackout drunk and I didn't even realize it."

"Right," Nate said. "Those kinds of drugs—and it's not just Rohypnol, there are other drugs that do the same kind of thing—they act quick and they empty out of your system quick. You don't know what's happening until it's over."

"And then you have to ask yourself whether you want to pay for the hospital visit," Anni said.

"Right," Nate said, relieved to have a chance to look at Anni again. "Yeah, it sucks that it costs so much to get health care."

"So you don't really see a lot of young women coming in and saying they were drugged," Larkin said, nudging Nate one more time.

"Not really," Nate said. Anni was about to say something, probably along the lines of "thank you," so Larkin kicked her again, not so hard this time. "Not really" didn't mean "no."

So they waited. Larkin sipped her bland hospital coffee and Anni stared at her cup of hospital tea and Nate picked his soda up and put it down again.

"We did get someone, earlier this year," Nate said. Finally. "It was a benzos thing, benzo abuse is really common right now, but I remember her saying that her boyfriend had done it. That he'd given her extra pills on purpose. Sorry, I shouldn't be telling you this."

"No, it's okay," Larkin said. It was exactly what she had hoped Nate would tell her.

"There wasn't any sign of assault," Nate said. "If I remember it right." He turned to Anni, because of course he would. "I don't want you to worry that there's someone out there crushing benzos into girls' drinks."

"I'm not worried," Anni said. Her shoulders were calm. Her hands were relaxed. Her eyebrow area was furious.

"You never are," Nate said, his face simultaneously adoring and impressed—no, intimidated. He had a crush on Anni and he was a little bit afraid of her. No wonder he had spent the entire visit twiddling with his soda bottle instead of drinking from it.

"Well, we don't want to keep you," Larkin said. "I know that you're probably busy."

She stood up; Anni immediately followed. Nate stayed seated. He was probably on his feet most of the day. "No, it was good to see you," he said, mostly to Anni. "Take care, okay?" He finally uncracked the top of his soda. "I don't want to have to take care of you. I mean, I do, I would, but—"

"I know what you mean," Anni said. Her generosity was quick, aimed directly at Nate's face, and gone as soon as she turned to Larkin. "We should go."

———

"Why were you glaring at me?" Larkin asked, once they were out of the hospital pavilion and walking towards the car.

"Because you could have gotten Nate fired," Anni said.

"He's not going to get fired," Larkin said.

"You're right, he's probably not," Anni said. They stood at the curb, waiting for the light to change. Anni's heels bounced up and down against the concrete. "But now he's going to ask me about that musical we're writing," she continued. "Every time he sees me."

"Awwww," Larkin said, "that's because he likes you."

"Well, I don't want him to like me," Anni said. "I mean, I don't want him to dislike me."

"But you don't want him to, like, *like* like you," Larkin said.

"Yes," Anni said. "I'm a single-like woman only. No double likes."

"Not by anyone?"

"That's a personal question," Anni said. "But no, since you asked."

"All right," Larkin said, clicking her key fob twice to unlock the car doors. "No double likes." She hadn't exactly been considering Anni as a romantic prospect—she hadn't even thought of it until that moment—but Larkin officially categorized her as *not an option.*

"But nobody gets that," Anni said, getting into the car. "They're always after me, my mom and my sister and everybody else, *Nate's so adorable, why can't you just like him, we all do, he's likeable and you're not, you're impossible, you need someone like Nate to calm you down, he already feels like part of the family.*"

Her answer was getting more personal by the minute. "And now I have to be extra-nice to him because we kind of lied to him. I mean, I didn't." She glared at Larkin again. "I didn't know you were going to."

"I didn't know I was either," Larkin said. "I've never done this before."

"So why did you do it?"

"I wanted to know what he knew," Larkin said. "So I created a situation in which he would tell us."

"Are you creating a situation with me right now?" Anni asked.

"No," Larkin said. "If anyone's creating anything right now, you are."

"How would I know, though?" Anni rubbed the backs of her shoes against the bottom of the passenger seat until they came off; she pulled her knees up to her chest and wrapped her arms around them. Her socks were printed with tiny candy corns. They also had individual toes. "I have trouble sometimes, with people. I couldn't tell if that story you told about getting blackout drunk was true, for example."

"It was true," Larkin said. "Part of it. I didn't tell all of it."

"I'm sorry," Anni said. "I'm assuming the part you didn't tell was worse."

"It was," Larkin said.

"People never tell the worst part," Anni said. She put her feet down and put her shoes and seatbelt on. "I guess that's what we have to get them to do."

Larkin pulled the car out of its parking spot. "I'll tell you the worst part, if you want." She flicked her turn signal, letting the ticking fill the car as she thought of how to say it. "I told that story to Nate as if it were something that someone else did to me. It wasn't." The car turned; the ticking stopped. "I knew exactly how much alcohol was in those drinks. I helped make them. Then I had two of them in a row with no food. I had already had dinner, and I was trying to lose weight, so it was mostly just a protein bar and a handful of jellybeans, which are surprisingly low calorie, and then I had these drinks and I kept not eating anything, I remember seeing the tray with vegetables and cheese cubes and dip and thinking *nope, not tonight, I have willpower,* and then I don't remember much of anything else until I was puking in my boyfriend's apartment."

They were at a stoplight; there were no other cars. Larkin glanced at Anni. "That's the worst part. I left out those details on purpose because I wanted Nate to give us more information."

"The light's green," Anni said.

"So if one of us is an impossible person," Larkin continued, "it isn't you."

"Drive," Anni said. "I mean, I shouldn't tell you what to do."

Larkin drove.

"My worst thing is also my best thing," Anni said. "I work best alone."

"We're working together now."

"No, we're not," Anni said. "As soon as you started talking to Nate, I stopped. You took over and I let you, because it was easier than trying to figure out how we could solve the problem in a way that satisfied both of us."

They were back at Anni's apartment building, the car parked and the air conditioning turned off, the sticky air beginning to leech through the car doors. "I'm a good accompanist and a good freelancer because I know exactly what my role is. Especially when there are contracts involved. I'm a terrible collaborator because I have no idea what the shiitake mushrooms I'm supposed to do when I'm with someone else and we're working together on the same thing at the same time."

One foot came up onto the seat; Anni flinched as soon as the shoe touched the upholstery and put it down again. "Also, I'm weird."

"Because you say *shiitake mushrooms* instead of *shit*?"

"No, that's because I have twin eight-year-old nephews," Anni said. "My sister prefers the kind of expletives that involve boogers and farts and fresh produce, and it's easier for me to run just one filter over my language than to create multiple filters for separate occasions."

She turned, looking directly at Larkin. "That's why I'm weird." Most people would have looked away.

"All right, now we know each other's worst thing," Larkin said, even though she was pretty sure that Anni still didn't know her worst thing because she hadn't actually said her worst thing. Just one part of one of the worst things she'd done that morning, and she wasn't even counting the barrette she still hadn't returned to her moth er's side of the bathroom. "It had to be Jessalyn, right?" In theater school she'd argued that someone could just change the subject without having an objective. "You saw the way she cried when she looked at Harrison, at that last rehearsal."

"That doesn't necessarily mean anything," Anni said. "She could have cried for all kinds of reasons."

"Sure," Larkin said, "but what if we tried to figure out whether it was because she thought Harrison—" She took a breath, which felt like it was made up of at least 81 percent water. "Do you want to know something weird about me, since we're getting personal? I was totally fine with playing let's-solve-a-murder, but now that there might be rape involved, it's like—"

"I know," Anni said. "Plus, it could mean that Jessalyn actually killed him."

"I can't imagine her killing anyone."

"Well, she might not have done it herself," Anni said. "Not physically. She would have just arranged everything so that he died naturally, from peanut poisoning. Assuming that's actually how he died, which is the question we'll try to answer on Monday."

"Great," Larkin said. "What are we going to do until then?"

"Practice our German," Anni said. "And try to find out whether Jessalyn or Harrison had access to benzodiazepines." She opened the car door. "And see if we can find out the answers to our questions without intentionally misleading people."

This time she did not look at Larkin when she said it.

CHAPTER 10

arkin did not practice her German. She said hello to her mother and went into the guest bedroom to toss her cardigan and blouse on the floor and place her mother's barrette carefully on the nightstand. Then she put on a T-shirt over her jeans and then she exchanged her jeans for pajama pants and then she got into bed and opened her laptop.

First her email, out of habit. Larkin still hadn't opened the most recent message from one of her student loan providers; she wasn't going to think about her loans until they were out of forbearance, which meant that she didn't have to think about them today. She also hadn't opened the message from Dr. Ed, reminding them of whatever he wanted to remind them about before Sunday's rehearsal with Maestro Kimbrough. She did open the message offering her 10 percent off on hoodies and joggers. Then she scrolled and scrolled and scrolled past images of cheap clothing that she couldn't afford and didn't even need— she had three hoodies rolled up in one of those cardboard boxes, not that it made any difference when her weather app was predicting temperatures in the mid-80s and humidity to match. She thought about finding a photo of Robert Preston as Harold Hill from *The Music Man*, giving him a speech balloon that read "I'm melting!" and posting it to social media. Then she decided that nobody would get it. None of her former classmates were in Iowa right now. They didn't know what it felt like.

Then Larkin searched "benzo poisoning" and read several depressing articles. She knew the Midwest had an opioid problem, it was one of the few things she had known about the Midwest before moving there, but she hadn't realized that people were also relying on benzodiazepines for pain management—and, in some cases, inadvertently or deliberately overdosing. That wasn't the information she was looking for, though. Larkin backspaced through "poisoning" and typed "date rape," wondering when the internet was going to decide she was a horrible person for wanting to know about this kind of stuff, but yes, benzos were occasionally used to—and then Larkin closed the tab.

So Harrison could have done it, if Harrison had wanted to do it. Or the woman whom Larkin currently assumed was Jessalyn could have been lying about it. Not if she'd gone to the hospital, though. That kind of thing takes too much time and costs too much money, even with insurance. So it had to be true. Or, at least, Larkin had to figure out if it were true. This meant—and Larkin asked herself what Anni would think of this and then decided she wouldn't ask—talking to Jessalyn, in a potentially misleading way. Finding out whether Jessalyn had been the person who went to the hospital. Finding out why Jessalyn thought it was Harrison who had drugged her.

And then—and Larkin's mind stumbled over the

thought like it was an unexpected crack in the sidewalk—finding out whether Jessalyn killed Harrison over it.

Because if Harrison were murdered, it would have had to have been by someone. A real person.

This whole thing was a mess, and she never should have gotten involved with it. Never should have started it. She should have left the entire thing to the cops, except for the part where she'd talked to the cops already and they didn't seem to think it was anything but a terrible accident. Which still could be true. The whole thing could be a terrible accident. Or her instincts, which she had been told to trust ever since her first acting class, could be correct. Someone murdered Harrison, and that person—well, she was going to find out who it was and then bring that person to justice. Because it was that easy, apparently. Because she, Larkin Day, could do it, even though she had not successfully done anything else with her life so far. Maybe because she had not successfully done anything else with her life so far.

That was her worst thing—the thing she had not been able to tell Anni in the car.

Larkin didn't know what to do next, so she let the internet decide for her. She tabbed over to her email again, because she couldn't remember if she'd had 48 unread messages or 49, and the 49th message turned out to be another one from Ed, but since the subject line read "Larkin, don't quit the choir," this time she opened it.

Hi, Larkin—

I wanted to thank you again for taking that check over to Anni's the other night. I also wanted to express my sincere hope that you stick with the chorale all the way through the perfor-mances—I know it would be easy to stop coming to rehearsals

*after everything that's happened, but if there's one thing I know
as a choral director it's that every voice counts.*

*Your mother told me about your struggles with the academic job market. Have you had the chance to get to know
Jessalyn Barnes yet? She also had a really rough time on the
market last year and I bet you two might have a lot to talk
about. I can introduce you at tomorrow's rehearsal if you want.
Another good reason to show up!*

Thanks, and see you soon?

Ed

Larkin did not want to talk to Jessalyn about the academic job market, but she did want to talk to Jessalyn—so
she replied *Thanks, an introduction would be great!* and then
backspaced and retyped the exclamation point a few times
and finally left it there.

After she sent the email, Larkin switched tabs and
pulled up the event she had created for her mother. She'd
added herself as a co-host when she created the event so
she could invite Anni; now she tapped "Claire Novak"
into the search field, hoping she hadn't guessed wrong.
There was Claire, grinning like a goofball at what
appeared to be some kind of police officers' pancake
breakfast. Larkin quickly scrolled through Claire's timeline, looking for any indication of a partner, but all she
found were pictures of Claire's golden retriever, Pal, and a
badly framed selfie in which Claire, her auburn hair pulled
back into a tiny ponytail, posed next to "a freshly washed
and detailed car!"

Claire also used social media to keep track of the books
she was currently reading, which seemed to be all of them.
Mira Grant, Terry Pratchett, Audrey Niffenegger, a couple
of cheesy romance novels with two women on the cover—
yep, Larkin had guessed nearly exactly right. She hoped

she had also guessed right about the look that had passed between Claire and her mother at the police station. And that her mother wouldn't be too judgmental about the fiction.

Larkin sent the message before she could change her mind.

Hi! This is going to sound odd, but my mother is throwing a party this Friday and she'd love for you to come. May I add you as a friend so I can pass along the invite?

Claire sent the thumbs-up emoji almost immediately.

CHAPTER 11

After the last rehearsal—the one that had been cut short, after Harrison's funeral—the corridorus seemed eager to get back into the singing spirit. Larkin arrived early, with the hopes of getting re-introduced to Jessalyn Barnes, and found that a good half of the choir was already there, setting up chairs and peeling plastic wrap off paper plates and baking pans. The snack-bringers appeared to have outdone themselves, and two of the altos were busy unfolding the metal legs from a fourth table.

Anni was at the Steinway, helping Gerald and Shawnta warm up. Ed was hovering, kind of pacing, near the podium where he no longer belonged. He was once again wearing his "this is my choir rehearsal shirt" T-shirt, this time under a college-branded hoodie that Larkin's mother also owned (it looked better on him). Several other singers had the same shirt and the same idea, the thick white lettering standing out and bringing the group together.

But none of those singers were Jessalyn, and Larkin began to regret the fifteen minutes she could have spent doing anything besides standing upstage left as a group of people who all knew what they should be doing got down to doing it. She tried to move a chair, to be helpful, but as soon as she unfolded it and stepped back someone else stepped in and moved it where it should have gone.

Then Ed saw her and waved, and then Larkin began walking around the chairs and their arrangers to say hello, but then one person sat down, and another, and ten, and twenty, and Larkin found herself standing, two rows ahead of her seat, receiving a silent stare from a man whom she assumed was either Beethoven reincarnated or, more likely, Maestro Kimbrough.

The rest of the choir was seated and silent. Maestro Kimbrough, who had ascended his podium with equal silence and gravitas, turned his gaze from Larkin and towards the assembled chorus. One move of his hand and they rose, a single sound of weight shifting and then several leftover sounds as Larkin squeezed her way back to her seat. Maestro Kimbrough waited. She didn't need to look at him to know that he, and the entire choir, were waiting.

But there she was, score in hand, realizing too late that everyone else had put their music in a black snakeskin folder. She saw Maestro Kimbrough register this, decide to ignore it—it was a choice he made, telegraphed under his bushy Beethovenian eyebrows so the whole choir understood—and then address the room.

"I am Maestro Kimbrough," he said, speaking both words as if he had no idea that they rhymed. "Thank you for being here. From the beginning."

Anni was two measures into the introduction when Maestro Kimbrough stopped conducting and directed his attention upstage left. "You are late to my rehearsal," he said, and the entire choir turned to look, and it was

Jessalyn. Larkin watched Jessalyn shift her eyes from Maestro Kimbrough to Ed, who said, "It's okay, she teaches on Sunday afternoons." Maestro Kimbrough said nothing except "We will begin again," and they did.

Now Larkin understood why Ed had emailed her and asked her not to quit the choir, because if she weren't already committed to sticking around long enough to find out whether one of the people in this room was secretly a murderer—and sure, it could be someone who wasn't in the room, but Larkin felt certain that if a murder had been done, it had been done in-house—she would have walked out again. Told Beethoven's Ghost to go *Götterfunken* himself, because she hated working with people who didn't treat people like *people*. He had the nerve—the *nerve!*—to turn to Anni after the initial run-through and say, because it was not a question, "Are you leaving out some of the notes?"

Anni held up her hands, fingers splayed. "Sorry, tiny hands." Then she realized he didn't get the joke. Maybe he didn't even get humor, as a concept. "I'll try to get more of the octaves, Maestro."

She's only had this gig for, like, three days! Larkin wanted to say. *She took it over because the former accompanist died, and he might even have been killed on purpose!* She wondered if the murderer would consider striking again.

Then Maestro Kimbrough stopped them a second time —well, more like a fifth time, but this was the second time he stopped to glare at the back corner of the room. "You are very late," he said. It was Marlene, her purse and folder clutched to her chest, her hands clutched together on top of them. Maestro Kimbrough looked again to Ed, waiting for yet another justification. "Come on in, Marlene," Ed said. "There's an empty seat next to Larkin."

Marlene took the seat and put her purse on it. They

continued singing, with no additional interruptions besides Maestro Kimbrough's. He gave excellent notes; short, specific comments that clarified exactly what needed to be adjusted, followed by an immediate opportunity to adjust it. But he did not praise them afterwards, the way Ed would have done. The only positive reinforcement was the opportunity to turn the page and keep going.

At exactly ninety minutes into the rehearsal, Maestro Kimbrough's phone beeped; he stopped them mid-measure and said, "Thank you, we will take a ten-minute break," and they did. Marlene, like many of the older megachoristers, took the opportunity to finally sit down.

"It looks like three other people brought scotcheroos today," Larkin said, because it looked like Marlene still hadn't gotten over the Maestro's reaction to her late arrival. "Won't be as good as yours, but nobody will be suffering from a lack of crisped rice."

Marlene's hands, which were already tightly interlaced, squeezed even tighter. The only thing that could fit between her palms was the vacuum of space. "I'm not going to be baking anymore," she said, eyes on her reddening fingers.

Larkin was going to say something pleasant, like "oh, you should," which sounded like the kind of thing a nice person from Iowa might say—even though she was neither of those—but Ed, who had decided to join them, beat her to it. "Don't let Maestro Kimbrough get you down," he told Marlene. "I've worked with him before. He says things quickly and he gets over things quickly."

"He probably doesn't even remember who you are," Larkin said. That was the kind of sentence that sounded nicer before she said it aloud.

"He probably doesn't," Ed agreed, his smile improving Larkin's sentiment. "Which is why we aren't going to forget you. I'm glad you're in the choir, Marlene." He turned. "You too, Larkin."

"Why did they pick this"—Larkin evaluated and discarded *asshole, jerkoff,* and *dillweed*—"guest conductor, when they could have had you?"

"I haven't studied orchestral conducting," Ed said. "And Maestro Kimbrough is one of the best at what he does."

"Sometimes being the best means being the best with people," Larkin said.

"Oh, come on," Ed said. "You've worked with musicians. We live our lives on either the downbeat or the afterbeat. Kimbrough's a downbeat guy."

"By which you mean he conducts with his hands because he's got his baton shoved up his butt," Larkin said. That, at least, got Marlene to relax a little—and speak. "No, he just wants to be like Stokowski."

Larkin didn't get the reference. "The conductor from *Fantasia*," Ed filled in, which was helpful in the sense that Larkin was aware that there was a movie called *Fantasia*. Hippos in tutus, which was a reference she got only because it had been made, in her direction, the one time her mother put her into a ballet class. It was time to change the subject. "You said you'd introduce me to Jessalyn."

"Yes, of course," Ed said. "I wanted Larkin to meet Jessalyn because they're both on the academic job market," he told Marlene. "Not competing for the same jobs, thank goodness."

"Jessalyn should have had that job," Marlene said. "The one Gerald got."

"It's a tough market," Ed said. "Lots of talented people." Then he scanned the room, indicated the direction they were going with a quick nod, and led Larkin towards the cluster of singers gathered near the snack tables. Jessalyn was standing with the other three soloists, pulling grapes off a linked brown stem.

"Excellent work this afternoon, everybody," Ed said, since whatever conversation they had been having stopped as soon as he arrived. "Jessalyn—do you know Larkin Day?"

"We walked in together," Jessalyn said, "a few rehearsals ago. We talked about good roles for altos."

"The world needs more good roles for altos," Shawnta said, raising an eyebrow.

"I'm *trying*," Ben said.

"Ben's writing an opera," Ed explained. He seemed to know, instinctively, when Larkin needed extra help. "But I wanted to introduce the two of you because you're both doing the academic job market thing—Larkin's in theater —and I thought you might, well I don't want to say *enjoy*, because there's nothing enjoyable about the academic job market, but, let's say, *value the opportunity to commiserate*."

"Thank god I don't have to play that game," Ben said.

"Thank god I don't want to," Shawnta echoed.

"Shawnta works at the library," Ed said, "and Ben—"

"I married well," Ben said.

"That's the polite way of putting it," Gerald said. He held one of those cookies that had a chocolate kiss in the center of it—Larkin couldn't remember what they were called—and bit the chocolate part out first. "Sugar daddy," he said to Larkin, before putting the rest of the cookie in his mouth.

"That's the impolite way of putting it," Ben said, and left the circle. Shawnta followed, and Ed said he wanted to grab a few treats before the second half of the rehearsal started. This left Jessalyn, Larkin, and Gerald.

"So how many times have you gone on the market?" Jessalyn asked. "This will be my second year. It took

Gerald two years to get his job, so maybe the second time's the charm, as they say."

Larkin did not want to say, but she did. "This'll be year four, for me."

"Oh," Jessalyn said, and Larkin understood what she meant, which was *you don't have a chance.* But her Iowa Friendly came through. "Well, if you ever want to swap CVs or something, let me know. I'm always glad to have an extra pair of eyes on my applications."

"Thanks," Larkin said. Then she thought of a way to get what she really wanted. "Hey, this is a silly question, but do you have a pencil sharpener? Mine broke, and I want to make sure I can take notes during the rest of the rehearsal." This was a lie; Larkin had yet to make a single pencil marking in her thick green score.

"Of course," Jessalyn said, leading Larkin away from Gerald and towards the four soloist chairs at the front of the room.

"I knew you would," Larkin said. She hadn't, really; it had been a toss-up between *pencil sharpener* and *tampon,* and she'd gone on instinct.

"It's a teacher thing," Jessalyn said, separating the gold handles of her apple-patterned knockoff purse and digging a hand inside. "Hang on, it's in here somewhere."

Then, as Larkin hoped she would, Jessalyn began pulling items out of her purse and setting them on the chair. A sunglasses case; a packet of tissues; a gold-handled, apple-patterned wallet. A slim, prescription-wrapped bottle of pills.

"Beta blockers," Jessalyn said. "Who doesn't have anxiety, right?"

"Sure," Larkin said. She had to find the exact right way to say this. "In grad school, we were all on beta blockers or benzos." Another lie; it had been Los Angeles, so they'd all had medical marijuana prescriptions. But the misdirection worked. Larkin saw Jessalyn flinch, her wrist recoiling against the faux leather of her purse, and then say, relatively calmly, "I tried benzos once. Didn't work out so well for me."

This was when Larkin would get to pull out "I'm sorry, I heard," just like she did with Carla, and then listen carefully to how Jessalyn responded—but that was also when Maestro Kimbrough returned from wherever guest conductors go during mandatory ten-minute breaks, and she didn't get the chance. She took the pencil sharpener that Jessalyn quickly pressed into her hand, and then quickly took her seat.

The second half of the rehearsal proceeded much like the first, with stretches of music interrupted by single sentences. Larkin took the directions without listening to them; at this point, despite the fact that she left her score in her car between rehearsals, she knew the movement well enough to spend most of it thinking about something else. Specifically, that bottle of pills that Jessalyn had pulled out of her bag. She needed to find a way to find out if Jessalyn was the patient that Nate had mentioned the other day, and if Harrison had somehow contributed to that whole situation, and if Jessalyn had retaliated by— well, that would be something, if she had. Murder. That was what it would be. Larkin had to keep reminding herself that this was a for-real mystery and not some long-form improv or LARP, even though she slipped right back into improv mode as soon as the rehearsal was over, walking right up to Jessalyn and saying "Here's your pencil sharpener back, thanks—and hey, if you want to get coffee sometime and talk about, like, how you got your adjunct gig, I would love to pick your brain." She couldn't believe she'd just said *pick your brain*. And to a potential murderer. "My treat." She couldn't believe she'd said that, either.

Jessalyn was not as good at improv as Larkin was. She must have done some acting at some point, probably had the lead in her high school musical, but it wouldn't have been a very complex lead. She would have played Sandy in *Grease*, Amalia in *She Loves Me*. Larkin understood all of this in the time it took Jessalyn to force a smile over the dark expression that had briefly crossed her face. "Of course," Jessalyn said, and they agreed that they would meet Tuesday morning at the coffee shop below Anni's apartment.

That was where both Larkin and Anni ended up, after rehearsal—not the coffee shop, but Anni's apartment, where they could talk without any of the other 148 megachoir members inadvertently overhearing. "So she was on benzos," Larkin explained, "and now she's on beta blockers. And we're going to meet on Tuesday, and I'm going to get her whole story."

"Are we going to feel bad that we might be asking someone to recount an assault she'd rather not talk about?" Anni asked, curled up on her sofa with another cup of poop tea.

"What if she does, though?" Larkin said. "Part of what I learned in my theater training is how to make a space for people to feel comfortable being emotionally honest. To share the truths about themselves, you know?"

"I thought theater was about being other people."

"You can't inhabit another person's emotional state until you get really familiar with your own emotions," Larkin said. "And I have spent the last I-don't-know-how-many years making a space for college students to get familiar with their emotions. All this training had better be good for something."

"Solving crimes?"

"I have such a hard time thinking of this as a crime," Larkin said. "I keep thinking of it as a mystery."

"Well, tomorrow we have the mystery of how to convince Sam Nagel to show us Harrison's death certificate," Anni said. "I can call his office in the morning and see when he's able to meet with us. Would tomorrow afternoon work for you, if I can get it set up?"

"Sure," Larkin said. At some point Anni would figure out that she had absolutely no plans for the majority of her time. "What are you going to say, though?"

"When you're calling a lawyer," Anni said, "you don't have to say anything. You just ask for a consultation. That gets you the meeting, and I'll let you take over from there."

CHAPTER 12

The law office was squidged between a spa and a photography studio; Larkin pulled into the parking lot to find Anni locking a blue and silver bike to a tree. "Someone should have thought to install bike racks," Anni said, swiveling the little numbers on her combination lock to foil potential thieves. "Otherwise, everyone will just keep driving forever."

"I don't think that's the only reason people drive." Larkin liked to use her car as her own personal karaoke booth, for example. It also made an excellent mobile storage unit. The trunk still contained at least six boxes that she hadn't yet moved into her mother's guest bedroom. "Wait—do you not drive? At all?"

"I can drive," Anni said. "At least I think I can. A few years ago I signed up for driving lessons just to make sure I still could, and I hadn't forgotten anything."

"But you don't have a car."

"Nope," Anni said. "I have a bike."

"Wait—how do you get to rehearsal?"

"Bike trail." Her blue and silver bike helmet was still

on her head; she pulled it off, clipped it around the strap of her canvas bag, and ran her hand through her cropped hair. "So how are we going to start this conversation? I still don't think it's going to work."

"It worked with your friend Nate," Larkin said. "All we have to do is stick as close to the truth as we can, and then keep quiet and listen."

So, once they were checked in at the reception desk and offered complimentary cups of coffee or water (Larkin took coffee, Anni took water), once Sam Nagel appeared and invited them to follow him down a hallway to what was in fact a wood-paneled, for-real lawyer's office, and once they were seated with their cardboard cups on law-firm-branded coasters and Anni's bag and bike helmet hanging off the back of her chair, Larkin said, "This is going to sound strange, but we're here because of Harrison."

"Ah," Sam Nagel said. He looked like the type of lawyer who should be on a commercial about lawyers. "I heard about that."

Larkin and Anni said absolutely nothing.

"I worked with Harrison when he was settling his parents' estate," he continued. "Poor guy."

Larkin and Anni stayed silent. Then Sam Nagel became suspiciously silent. Larkin wondered if he was on to them.

"We want to know how Harrison died," Anni said, suddenly. "We're curious if you can help us confirm whether it was because of his peanut allergy."

She reached into her bag, her helmet smacking awkwardly against the well-varnished chair, and pulled out a business card. "I'm a writer, mostly in finance, I also write for life insurance companies, and I'm thinking about pitching a story on people who have life-threatening allergies as adults. We think of peanut allergies as this thing that kids have, right? But I saw Harrison collapse once, at a rehearsal, after eating something that someone had brought as a treat and didn't label correctly. He had to go to the emergency room."

"I've got a kid with a peanut allergy," Sam said. "Terrible thing."

"I know," Anni said, and Larkin wondered how she'd figured that out. Larkin had checked Sam's social media accounts before the meeting, as part of what she was now considering her standard pre-investigation research, but all his posts were promotional and professional. "That's why this story's going to be so important," Anni continued. "The cost of living with a peanut allergy as an adult, the precautions you have to take, and so on."

"Well, I'd be happy to talk to you about what my wife and I are doing, for our son," Sam said, "but I'm not sure how I can help with Harrison."

"The obituary didn't say how he died," Anni said. "But the death certificate would confirm anaphylaxis. If you could get it for us. For the story."

"Oh," Sam said. "I see. You want me—"

"To contact the department of public health and request a copy of the death certificate," Anni said. Larkin would have let him finish.

Sam laughed. It sounded the way his office looked; quiet and calm and highly polished. It was not unkind, but it was the equivalent of a firmly closed door. "You know I can't do that," he said, and Anni's face blanched with shame. "You knew it when you came in here."

Larkin called up the foolish, innocent character she had put on for Carla. "They say it never hurts to ask. We were just hoping—"

"Wait, how are you part of this?" If Sam wasn't suspicious of them before, he was now. "I don't know what you kids are after, but please don't waste any more of my time."

"You can bill me for it," Anni said, standing up, grabbing her bike helmet, dropping it. "My address is on the card," she said, crouching on the floor to pull her helmet out from under her chair. Then she put it on, snapped the clasp under her chin, and walked out the door.

"Sorry," Larkin said, before following Anni out of the office and through the lobby and into the parking lot. The air felt like a hundred wet sweaters, but the look Anni gave her could have dried them, shrunk them up, and set them all on fire.

"I told you," Anni said, fumbling with her bike lock. "I knew this wouldn't work."

"So we try something else," Larkin said. "Maybe we pretend to be Harrison's relatives. Aren't we all brothers and sisters under Christ or something?"

"I am not pretending anything anymore." Anni turned on two sets of blinking, blinding bike lights. "I lied to a lawyer. I mean, I didn't technically lie, because I only said I was thinking about pitching the story, but I still disrespected the ethics of my profession."

"What, you mean telling people they can get out of debt if they make a budget?" Larkin had read a few of Anni's articles. Most of them were variations on what seemed to be obvious—if you want to get out of debt, figure out how to put more money towards your credit card balances; if you want to make a will, *make one*—and then Larkin had closed the tabs without putting any of Anni's good advice into practice.

"You don't think there are ethics in that kind of work? You don't think I don't *do the math* on whether the Snowball Method is better than the Avalanche Method? That I just make it all up and collect my paycheck?"

Anni tightened the strap on her bag until it lay flat against her back. "That lawyer could email my clients," she continued. "Or he could go on social media. He could tell everyone that I contacted him under false pretenses."

"So make them real pretenses," Larkin said. "Write the article about the peanut butter thing. How did you figure that out, anyway?"

"He had an epinephrine injector in his desk. I saw it when he took out the coasters." Anni swung one leg over her bike. "You know that's probably how Harrison died, right? An ordinary allergic reaction. If it had been something else, the medical examiner would have found it during the autopsy."

"Maybe he wasn't autopsied."

"Did you do absolutely zero research before you started this murder hunt? You have to autopsy people if they die under unexpected circumstances. It's on the Iowa Department of Public Health website."

Larkin hadn't even known there was an Iowa Department of Public Health, much less that it had the website that apparently contained all the death rules. "I did plenty of research," she said. "In-person research. With Carla and Jessalyn and Nate."

"By lying to them!"

"We could still—"

"Do not say we could still write a musical together," Anni said, her toes bouncing back and forth against the grass as she straddled her bike. "I'm not going to do this anymore. Harrison is dead and he might have been a creep and there's nothing we can do about any of that and *that's it.*"

She waddle-walked her bike across the sidewalk and off the curb. "Also, we're not kids. I'm 37. That's practically pushing 40."

Then she rode away.

———

Larkin was expecting to get back to her mother's house, grab the bag of red licorice out of the cupboard, change out of her ridiculous floral blouse that she hated, look up the department of health or whatever online, and figure out how to get Harrison's death certificate on her own. She was not expecting to find her mother waiting for her in the kitchen.

"Larkin," her mother said.

"Hey, Mom. You're back early!" Something about her mother didn't look right. The tension in her shoulders. The grit of her jaw. The fact that she had fists instead of hands.

"I thought I might have lunch with my daughter," Josephine said. "And then I got a very interesting message. Do you know who it was from?"

Larkin knew this was a trap. Josephine rarely fell into the typical mother clichés, but using sing-song sweetness as a prelude to anger was one of them. Not that it looked like Larkin would get much of a prelude.

"No," Larkin said, all innocence. She really didn't know. "Who was it?"

"Claire Novak."

Oh.

"She said you had invited her to our party on Friday."

"You said I could invite my friends." Larkin rarely fell into the typical daughter clichés, but pulling at the loopholes in her mother's rules was one of them.

"She's your friend?"

"She's yours."

"She's not."

"Well, she could be," Larkin said. "I think she wants to be."

"That's fine," Josephine said—and once again Larkin swore she saw her mother's face soften, just for a moment—"but that doesn't mean you can invite her to an academic party."

"How is it an academic party?"

"Did you pay any attention to the people on the invite list?" Larkin hadn't; they were just names that she'd typed into a search bar. "Do you pay any attention to anything you do?"

That was taking it a little too far. "Yes, I do!" Larkin said, her voice rising. "Everyone says I don't, but I do pay attention! I know you have a thing for Officer Novak, and I know she has a thing for you, and I'm sorry I didn't realize it was some party for the people you worked with, but when you invite people to something on social media you don't see the part of their profile where they list their fancy-schmancy real person jobs!" That wasn't how she had expected that part of the sentence to go. "You just see their name and their face, which you would know if you paid attention to how the internet works!"

"I don't care how the internet works!"

"Rallying cry of your generation." Now Larkin knew she'd taken it too far.

"I care that my daughter felt the need to invade herself into my love life—I mean my private life. That is not an area of your concern, nor is it an area in which you should insert yourself."

Larkin's mother's love life had been an area of Larkin's concern ever since Larkin had been old enough to understand that she had not only a mother but also a father, and her mother and her father had once been married, and all of that had ended before she'd been able to turn any of it into memories. But Larkin knew that it was not the right time to bring that up. Instead, she said "I'm sorry."

"I don't insert myself in your life," Josephine continued.

"Yes, you do," Larkin said. "You're making me go to that interview tomorrow."

"I'm not making you do anything."

"Well, what would you have said if I had told you to cancel it?"

Josephine shifted her gaze away from Larkin—then back on, with the full force of the Mother Guilt Stare. "I would have told you that you were wasting an opportunity, and that you needed to think seriously about your priorities and your path towards independence."

"By which you mean, when am I getting the fuck out of your house."

Larkin watched her mother absorb what she had just said. "You are always welcome in my home," Josephine told her, her voice slow and careful. "But I think it would be a good idea if you spent the rest of the day somewhere else."

"I'm sorry," Larkin said again.

"I know," her mother said. "Let's just give each other a little break. I'll see you for dinner."

CHAPTER 13

Larkin didn't know where she would go, at first; she thought about the coffee shop, but she didn't want to accidentally run into Anni—and she really didn't want to pay for a coffee. She'd grabbed her laptop and a granola bar before leaving her mother's house, and at first she drove aimlessly: past the coffee shop, past the college, and onto the highway. The road signs pointed towards the corridor she was currently stuck in and the airport that could get her out of it, not that she had enough money on any of her credit cards to pay for a plane ticket, not that she knew where she would go. Back to Los Angeles? Give New York another try? Her life was already garbage, so she might as well pick between rain-soaked garbage and subways and urine-soaked garbage and sunshine.

Then her fuel light turned on.

That was the end of her escapist plans. Larkin couldn't afford to waste any more gas, not when she wasn't sure she could trust any of her credit cards to buy her another tank; she took the nearest exit, crossed the Cedar River, drove past the orchestra hall into downtown Cedar Rapids, and parked her car in front of the one place she knew she could visit for free.

The public library.

Larkin had not yet visited any of the library branches within the Metro Library Network, though her mother had been urging her to check them out. The Cedar Rapids library building was nicer than the libraries she used to visit in Los Angeles, with floor-to-ceiling windows and one of those ubiquitous red metal sculptures taking up half of the front lawn. It sat across from the Cedar Rapids Art Museum, with a park in between; Larkin saw strollers and parents and flowers and fountains and one man in a shabby overcoat sleeping on a bench. There were a few people sleeping inside the library as well, with their duffels and backpacks and black plastic trash bags next to the chairs, but this wasn't the kind of library Larkin had become familiar with in her former big-city life, where you walked in and grabbed your books and tried to avoid making eye contact with anyone. This was a library that people *used*, for both its original purpose and its subsequent ones. There were toddlers running around and old people chatting next to the café and a young woman in a summer dress running a stack of paperbacks through the self-checkout. Upstairs, there were rows of heads bent over library computers, people learning and teaching English in study carrels, and one man bravely plodding along at a treadmill desk.

And then there was Shawnta.

She was wearing a red lanyard and a T-shirt printed with the names of banned books, and when she saw Larkin, she smiled. Larkin wasn't sure whether that smile was genuine or whether it was a service worker thing, but it was one of the few smiles she had gotten that day—so she took it, and said hello.

"You're in the chorale, right?" Shawnta said.

"Yeah," Larkin said. She didn't tell Shawnta that they had already technically met. "One of the altos."

"Team Alto," Shawnta said. "Best part of the choir."

"I don't know," Larkin said, returning the compliment. "I'd say those soloists are pretty good."

"We're getting there," Shawnta said. "Our first soloist rehearsal was terrible. I had never seen Ed look so stressed out."

"Well, it was the first rehearsal." She didn't tell Shawnta she had been through a few of those herself.

"No, it was a disaster," Shawnta said, with a warm, deep alto laugh. "Jessalyn brought her boo, which, fine, he's adorable, but that is not the place, and then Gerald was being his usual pleasant self, the bitchiest straight man I know, and Ben could barely sing 'cause he'd just finished playing Henry Higgins in *My Fair Lady*—"

"And that part isn't even for a singer," Larkin joked.

"Right?" Shawnta laughed again. "And then Harrison, not to speak ill of the dead, came back from the break looking like he had shit his pants or something. Could barely hold it together, missing notes left and right, and there's Ed being all Mister Conductor Cheerleader, waving his baton like a pom-pom and trying to look like he's not going to cry."

Larkin felt sorry for Ed. "Well, you all got better."

"That's what we do," Shawnta said. This time her smile was less service-worker and more human. "It's good to see you," she said, and Larkin smiled and said, "Good to see you too," and she was all the way down the stairs before she put together what Shawnta had said in between everything else she'd said. Harrison had barely been able to hold it together—when would that have been? Larkin took an empty chair at the end of the computer table, opened her laptop, logged onto the library's free Wi-Fi, and waited impatiently for her email to load. There'd been an email, about the schedule. There it was. *Sunday, September 18: Soloists only.*

That was the week when Harrison was supposed to have called her. The week she'd spent waiting by her phone and trying not to hate him. The last week of Harrison's life.

Larkin opened a new email because that was the fastest way she could think of to get something she could type in. Then she began writing:

SEPTEMBER 18 SOLOIST REHEARSAL
SEPTEMBER 22 FULL CHOIR REHEARSAL,
HARRISON DIES

She'd had to count on her fingers to get to September 22, and she stared at the two lines of text as if they would somehow become one of those crime-scene timelines where everything was connected in red thread. Then she kept typing.

WHEN WAS BENZO GIRL
WHEN DID JESSALYN SWITCH TO BETA
BLOCKERS
WHY WAS HARRISON UNABLE TO HOLD IT
TOGETHER

Larkin glanced at the people around her, hoping nobody would be interested enough in her laptop screen to start reading it. The man on her left appeared to be absorbed in online job ads, the man on her right, in online porn. There were two kids crammed into a single chair, watching videos of other kids playing video games. She minimized her email and opened a new tab.

Jessalyn Barnes. There she was, on every social media platform in existence, cross-posting inspirational quotes and outfit selfies and vacation photos. She had been part of a Cedar Rapids chamber group that had spent a month touring Europe, a few summers ago—there she was at Westminster Cathedral, there she was at St. Mark's Square, there she was at a pizzeria with Gerald and Shawnta and Ben and an older man with a rich-person tan and an extremely-rich-person watch who Larkin assumed was Ben's husband.

I like the Eiffel Tower photo the best, someone named Rosalyn Barnes had commented.

There was no photo of Jessalyn at the Eiffel Tower. The chamber choir seemed to have hit every other major tourist trap but that one—and then Larkin noticed that some of the photos in Jessalyn's Europe series had originally been posted on Ben's timeline, they'd only ended up on Jessalyn's because he'd tagged her, so Larkin went to Ben's profile and opened up all his photos at once, until she saw it.

The Eiffel Tower, at night. Ben and his silver fox, and Jessalyn and Harrison. Two embraces, two feet kicked up as Ben and Jessalyn looked adoringly at their respective boos, as Shawnta would say. Rosalyn Barnes had left a comment that consisted of three sparkling hearts.

This photo was not on Jessalyn's timeline. Not any photos of Jessalyn and Harrison, not on any of her social media accounts.

There was also a recent gap in her posting, one that you might not notice unless you knew to look for it—and yet there it was, Jessalyn had essentially absented herself from all of her formerly active accounts between Memorial Day and Labor Day, which Larkin could have written off as one of those social media detox things except Jessalyn hadn't written one of those obligatory posts explaining why she was taking a social media detox. Instead, she went from yet another outfit selfie—"New suit, who dis?"—to a photo in which she was posing side by side with the man who had accompanied her to the funeral. He was holding a pitchfork, and it didn't look like Jessalyn had made him do it; they were relaxed, happy, comfortable in each other's presence. It was one of the rare photos where you could only gauge their true emotions by covering up the bottom halves of each face; their lips were clamped into fake frowns, but their eyes were smiling.

Rosalyn, who had to be Jessalyn's mother because she both liked and commented on everything Jessalyn posted—Larkin's mother never did that, Josephine believed that excessive praise discouraged self-reliance and discredited the parent—had replied with "I love seeing you so happy," followed by the paintbrush emoji and a smiley face with heart eyes. Ben had also left a comment, noting that the couple in *American Gothic* were actually supposed to be a father and daughter and providing a link to an article explaining the whole deal. Larkin skipped the article and skimmed the rest of Jessalyn's profile for any hints about recent prescription changes. She wasn't expecting any, at this point; Jessalyn's online presentation seemed cultivated to present a self she hoped would exist someday, and that person was definitely not going to share stories about her anxiety medication.

Or her trip to the hospital, if Larkin's instincts were correct. Another type of person would have turned the experience into advocacy, adding #metoo to their social media posts and urging people to donate to their local rape crisis center. But the woman whom Harrison might have deliberately drugged did not present with any signs of assault, and someone like Jessalyn—if it had in fact been Jessalyn—could have decided that the person she wanted to become would never, ever mention it.

Unless, of course, someone like Larkin—who had been trained to help theater students access their unmentioned, uncultivated emotions—could get her to bring it up.

Larkin looked at the two photos of Jessalyn—the ones separated by a summer of social-media silence—one more time. A new outfit, a new beau. Two different poses, no other clues. Not that Larkin was expecting there to be clues, the way there were in the mystery novels that took up an entire section of the library.

But it would be nice if she could uncover at least one.

CHAPTER 14

arkin knew that her mother had signed her up for an 8:30 a.m. job interview before the two of them had fallen into their largely un-commented-upon conflict, in the sense that neither of them were really talking to each other except to say the kind of bland, polite courtesies that were intended to assure the other that they were still loved, deep down, underneath all of the anger. They spent all of Monday night, plus the part of Tuesday that Larkin still thought was too early to be considered *morning*, avoiding each other in the kitchen and the bathroom—except to say "excuse me" and "thank you for making the coffee" and, as Larkin's mother had said before Larkin left the house, "I hope you have a good interview."

Nothing could be good about an interview that Larkin didn't want, for a job she didn't want, during a part of the day in which nobody should actually be *working*, while wearing an armpit-scented suit that fit so badly that she'd had to loop a hair tie through the buttonhole on her pants. Although her mother had not set any of this up as a result of their fight—if anything, the interview was one of its instigators—it still felt like a punishment. Larkin was being anti-grounded: told to leave the nest and report to duty and strike out on her own (she couldn't come up with anything but clichés this early).

The administrative assistant whom Larkin might be replacing did not offer Larkin any coffee. Instead, she let Larkin sit in a black plastic chair while she fielded phone calls, typed rapidly at her computer, and kept the copy machine continuously running. Larkin wondered if she was even qualified to take over this woman's position, even for two months. She could type fast enough, but she hadn't touched a phone that wasn't attached to a pocket-sized supercomputer in years.

And then she was called into another office, and introduced to a couple of people who said nice things about her mother, and asked why she was interested in the job.

Larkin wasn't expecting this question. Well, she was expecting it at some point, but not right out the gate (clichés, again). She was supposed to tell them a little bit about herself first, set the room at ease with stories of her ambition and competencies. Instead, she said "Because my mom said I needed to get a job."

"You know this is just a short-term position," one of her interviewers told her. "To cover a twelve-week maternity leave."

"Yes," Larkin said. "That's why I'm interested in it." Good. "Because I don't want to do this kind of thing forever." Bad, bad, bad. "I mean, I'm currently working on my dissertation." Better? Larkin tried to recall how her interviewers had been introduced. She realized that none of the people at the table were faculty; that they were all administrative assistants and HR associates who might very well want to do this kind of thing forever.

"Larkin, can you talk us through your resume? Have you done administrative work before?"

Larkin had been ready, when she came in, to say something ease-setting about how anyone could make photocopies, and how she'd made plenty of them when she was working for various theater directors in New York. Now she was pretty sure her name-dropping wouldn't impress and her joke wouldn't land. "I haven't worked the kind of admin job that's behind a desk," she said. "I've been an assistant director and an assistant stage manager, both of which require a substantive amount of support work including taking notes, typing and distributing those notes, making copies, running errands, and so on. But no, I have not had a job like this before." She added, as convincingly as she could, "I am eager to learn."

"Well, we were hoping to get someone with a little more experience," another interviewer told her, "but your mother said you were as sharp as a tack" (apparently everybody thought in clichés at this time of day). "Of course we're interviewing a few other people"—and Larkin knew she hadn't gotten the job—"but we'll let you know."

They stood, Larkin stood, hands were shook, smiles went all around. Then Larkin was escorted outside, into a brilliantly warm October day, the air like a thousand spiderwebs clinging to her skin. It was 8:52 a.m. and she had no idea what she was going to do with herself—for the next ten minutes or, if she was honest with herself, the next ten years.

Then she heard a familiar voice call her name.

"Larkin!"

It was Ed, waving and smiling. Larkin hadn't considered that she might run into Ed, but of course it made sense; this was his campus, just like it was her mother's.

Just like it would never be hers. Larkin waved back, but did not smile.

"What are you doing here?" Ed asked. He was dressed for professorial success in a crisp collared shirt and khakis, and Larkin felt embarrassed that she hadn't bothered to iron the blouse that was currently hiding the rubber band on her pants. She'd sprayed it down with wrinkle releaser, which had released a cloying floral smell but not much else.

"My mom made me do this interview," Larkin said, and then wished she'd found a way to phrase it that didn't make her sound twelve years old. "I mean, she strongly suggested I interview for this temporary admin position, to cover a maternity leave."

"Oh, that's Madison," Ed said. "She's great. I'm sure you'd be great, too."

"No, I wouldn't," Larkin said. "I'd be terrible at that job. I was very terrible at the interview." She looked at Ed, who was still smiling at her, and decided to be honest. "I'm so embarrassed about the whole thing. That my mom had to get me an interview, that it was for a job I couldn't have done even if I'd wanted it, and that I had to get up early and put on this suit that makes me look awful and, you know, *fail.*"

"I wouldn't say that you'd failed," Ed said. "You learned that you might not want to pursue a career in office administration."

"I already knew that."

"You learned that maybe you don't need to wear that suit next time."

"Hey," Larkin said, her smile inching a bit wider. "Only I get to say bad things about my suit."

"You learned that your mom cares about you enough to try to help you succeed."

Larkin's smile fell. "My mom and I are not in a good place right now. I kinda screwed things up with her too. We haven't really talked in two days, except to say, like, *would you like some more coffee.*"

"I'm surprised you have to ask," Ed said. "I've seen your mother with her coffee."

"Yeah, well, I want to say I'm sorry, and I don't think she wants me to say anything," Larkin said. "I've been trying to stay out of the house, but I'm running out of places to go, and I'm trying to work on my dissertation, and *that* is going nowhere, and I'm trying to figure out—"

Larkin stopped herself from saying *whether Harrison was murdered*. Ed was still looking at her, listening, so she picked a different truth instead. "What I'm going to do with the rest of my life."

"Well, I can't help you with the rest of your life, but I've got a bunch of music to organize if you need something to do for the next few hours. I can't pay you, but I can treat you to a cup of coffee. The coffee gene is matrilineal, right?"

Larkin was impressed that Ed was able to pull out *matrilineal* at 8:58 in the morning. He was surprising—he was continually surprising—and Larkin found herself agreeing to his offer.

"I should warn you that it's not going to be the best cup of coffee, because it's the free stuff they serve in the music office, but you can have as much of it as you want." Ed smiled again—he hadn't ever stopped smiling, really—and led Larkin across the quad and into the Center for Performing Arts.

Inside it was exactly like every other performing arts building Larkin had ever been in: the hall filled with production posters and audition notices, the lobby where students piled onto torn-up couches and broke into song, the basement with rows of instrument lockers and practice rooms and ad-hoc rehearsal spaces. It smelled like valve oil and feet, and Larkin took a sip of the bitter cup of coffee Ed had poured for her, because everything else around her was so familiar it hurt.

Then she sloshed half of her coffee down her blouse.

"It is not my day," Larkin said. She rubbed her foot against the few drops of coffee that had fallen onto the tile floor, in the hopes that they would get absorbed into the sole of her shoe or something.

"Do you want to—" Ed paused. "Wow, there is no way I can ask this question without violating some moral turpitude clause."

"Are you asking me whether I want to take my shirt off?" Larkin had never seen Ed look flustered before. It was amusing.

"How about we say *change your clothes*?"

So that was how Larkin ended up wearing Ed's "this is my working out at the YMCA T-shirt" over her suit pants, while the two of them sat on the floor of the choir library, pulling sheet music out of manila folders and putting individual pieces into piles. It was also how Larkin learned Ed's history: he'd grown up in St. Louis, studied vocal music and choral conducting in Cincinnati, and gotten his DMA in Los Angeles because—as he put it—"I'd always wanted to see the ocean."

"I ended up in L.A. because I needed a school that didn't have a foreign language requirement," Larkin said. "I could tell you six different things your body language is communicating right now, but I never took the time to learn French. Or Russian, which would have been useful for my dissertation. Or Spanish, which just would have been useful."

"Okay," Ed said. "Tell me six different things my body

language is communicating right now."

"Whoooo," Larkin said. "All right. Um. . . well, you're sitting on your heels. That's a position you can get up and down from fairly quickly. Your hands are relaxed, you're not clenching or gripping or wringing, but you're carrying some tension in your shoulders. That suggests that you're comfortable in this situation, but you're also a little on your guard. You're expecting to need to spring to your feet at any moment and defend the fact that you have an unemployed, unsanctioned woman in the supply closet—

"Choir library—"

"Helping you sort all of this music," Larkin continued. "So that's making you just a little bit nervous, probably because you don't have tenure yet and are still worried that you're going to do something wrong and screw everything up."

"I'm not worried about tenure."

"That's the first time you've lied to me this entire morning," Larkin said. "I could tell because you raised your eyebrows to try to look honest. But you're also smiling, and that part's genuine. You've got the eye crinkles going on. And you could say that it's just because I'm telling you this hilarious story about your body language, but you've been smiling this entire time. Which means that you are currently the only person in Pratincola who is happy to have me around."

Then Larkin counted, on her fingers. "Yep, that's five things."

"You said six things."

Larkin looked at Ed, first all over his face and then into his deep brown eyes. His pupils were larger than they'd been a second ago. She could hear his breathing; his heartrate had gone up. So had hers. She knew what it all meant, or could mean. She felt her cheeks flush, and then her neck and chest, everything that was currently covered by Ed's T-shirt.

"I can't think of a sixth one," she said. It was the first time she'd lied to him that entire morning.

They let the truth dissipate, heartbeats slowing down and pupils closing up, and then Ed said, casually, "Do you like living in Pratincola?"

"No," Larkin said. "Do you?"

"Well, I bought the T-shirt," Ed said. His smile was different, this time. Like he had chosen not to put all of himself into it.

"Sure, but isn't this, like, a temporary stop for you?"

"Before what?" Ed got up and started putting the sorted choral music into file cabinets.

"I don't know, something bigger and better?" Larkin stayed where she was, passing stacks of sheet music to Ed. "More diverse?"

"I grew up in the Midwest," Ed said. "It's my home too."

"Sorry," Larkin said. "That was presumptuous of me."

"Don't worry about it."

"Well, the Midwest isn't my home," Larkin said. "I don't know how it is here yet."

———

Larkin went back to her mother's home for lunch, because she wasn't going to ask Ed to treat her and she didn't have the money to treat herself. After she and Ed had looked at each other and mutually agreed not to comment on what they saw, the conversation had grown stagnant; it had been a relief when Ed had said that he needed to get ready for his next class. Larkin was still wearing Ed's T-shirt, her own coffee-stained blouse sloppily folded and tucked into the leather portfolio that also contained two cream-colored copies of her resume. She had told Ed she'd wash his shirt and bring it to the next rehearsal.

In other words, they had promised to meet again.

But first Larkin had to get the shirt off her body and into the washing machine without her mother asking her whether she'd joined the YMCA. She got as far as the kitchen—and although Larkin had hoped her mother would be in her office or at the campus dining hall or literally anywhere else, she realized, as soon as Josephine looked up from her laptop, that she was glad to see her there. She was also glad that her suit jacket covered the majority of what she wasn't supposed to be wearing.

"How did the interview go?"

"It was fine," Larkin said. Her mother must have come home specifically to ask—which didn't irritate Larkin as much as it would have, even three hours ago. "I didn't get the job."

"You don't know that."

Larkin wondered how long her mother had been waiting at the kitchen table. If she'd gone into the office at all. "Yes, I do. They want someone with more administrative experience."

"Did you tell them—"

"Yes," Larkin said. "I told them I could learn, I said I was eager, I did all the things, and I didn't get the job. And that's fine." It really was, in a way that it hadn't been before Larkin had spent the morning with Ed. "And I wanted to say that I was sorry. For inviting Claire to the party."

Larkin knew, even before her mother spoke, that she was forgiven. "I'm sorry, too. For setting up the interview without asking."

"It turned out okay, though," Larkin said. "I ended up

running into Ed. I mean, Dr. Jackson."

"I know who Ed is," Josephine said. "I helped hire him."

Larkin had been just about to ask her mother what she thought about Ed, and how long she'd known him, and whether she thought he was smart and funny and interesting, and whether the rule about *directors not kissing the people they direct* could be broken since Maestro Kimbrough was technically in charge of the choir now. But she couldn't ask any of that, because if her mother agreed with it all and she and Ed did end up dating and then they broke up, it could affect Ed's job. His tenure file. His entire career.

"Well, we had a good talk," she said instead.

"I just had a good talk too," her mother said. "On the computer. With Claire."

"You did not!"

"Yes, I did," Josephine said, her voice tinged with just a bit of triumph. "She's kind of a fascinating woman."

"Is she?" Larkin teased, sitting down at the table next to her mother. "Do I get any credit for setting the two of you up?"

"Of course not. I don't want to encourage that kind of behavior."

"You've never encouraged any of my behavior," Larkin said. "All you've ever done is tell me to *pay more attention to the details.*"

"I think that counts as encouragement," Josephine said. "Especially in the Adlerian sense."

Larkin heard *Ed*lerian, not *Ad*lerian, and automatically clamped her folder over the parts of Ed's T-shirt that were not currently covered by her suit jacket. This, unfortunately, drew focus to the one detail she was hoping her mother would not pay attention to.

"What are you wearing?"

"I spilled coffee on my interview blouse," Larkin said, not moving the folder away from her chest. "Luckily I still had a bunch of old T-shirts in the back of the car."

"Hmmm," Larkin's mother said. She looked at her laptop and tried to pretend that she wasn't looking at her daughter. Larkin hugged her folder like it was a transitional object and tried to think of a better transition. "Do you want some more coffee? I think I'll make some after I go change into something more comfortable."

That, unfortunately, only called even more attention to her clothing. "I've seen that shirt before," Larkin's mother said. "It came from Raygun, that store downtown. I had them make one that read *this is my strategic planning T-shirt* for an academic retreat a few years ago."

"How'd the retreat go? Did you get your strats planned?"

"How'd you get a Raygun T-shirt in the back of your car?"

Sometimes Larkin's mother was very good at being a mother.

"Okay, fine." Larkin said. "Ed loaned me his shirt because I was, like, dripping with coffee." She opened her folder to show her mother the ruined blouse. "See, it's still wet."

"I do see," Josephine said. She ran her fingers over a damp spot on one of Larkin's resumes. "On the subject of my not encouraging you often enough," she continued, slowly, "you understand why I'm not going to encourage you to spend more time with Dr. Jackson."

"Yeah," Larkin said. "I get it."

"But I'm not going to discourage it either," Larkin's mother said, twitching her nose.

CHAPTER 15

The woman behind the counter smiled as Larkin approached. "Good to see you again!" Of all the things Larkin did not want to be, a regular at a Pratincola coffee shop was a lot closer to the top of her list than she realized—and yet she found herself saying "good to see you as well," and then, instead of leaving it at that, "I really like those glasses." Baristas always seemed to know where to find the best glasses.

"Thanks," the woman said. "I woke up a little later than usual this morning, so I just threw them on!" Of course she did. She probably just threw on her V-neck pocket tee, too, and it still looked ten times better than Larkin's dress-for-investigatory-success outfit. Larkin only felt like herself when she was wearing all black, but here she was in the kind of sleeveless polyester blouse that she was pretty sure was actually called a "shell," paired with the top half of yesterday's interview suit and her least-worn-out jeans. Plus her mother's barrette, still not returned to the shared bathroom. As soon as she got this murder solved and her dissertation finished and her life back on track, she would buy all new clothes.

But first she had to successfully buy a cup of coffee.

"It looks like your card isn't going through?" The barista, out of kindness, made it sound like a question.

Larkin had known this would happen at some point, and had deliberately avoided looking at her credit card app so she wouldn't know when that point would be. She opened up her wallet to see if another credit card would be willing to spot her on a $3.99 pumpkin pie latte—the daily special, it had house-made pie crust crumbles on top of the whipped cream—and then she heard a very familiar soprano.

"Oh, I've got it." It was Jessalyn, pulling out her credit card, saying something cheerful about how Larkin could treat her to coffee the next time. "I know what it's like when you're job hunting."

"Aren't you still job hunting?" Larkin asked, as they carried one black coffee with honey and one pumpkin pie latte back to the table at which Larkin had previously inter-rogated Carla Ramirez Buckholtz. Unlike Carla, Jessalyn walked right into the conversational trap Larkin had set, squeezing herself against the corner of the coffee shop and giving herself nowhere to look but Larkin's inquisitive eyes.

"I don't know," Jessalyn said. "I kind of like building my own voice studio. I'm still sending out CVs, of course, but the whole academic market is so stressful, and some-times when the path is hard it means you're going in the wrong direction." She took a sip of her coffee; the mug came down without a single lipstick stain, even though Larkin had already managed to get lipstick marks into her whipped cream. "Remember, it's all about finding your unique voice, and learning what you can do with it."

Jessalyn smiled. Then she blushed. "Plus, I kinda met someone."

This someone was named Adam, and he had a family farm, and according to Jessalyn he was the kind of person who was worth giving up an entire career for. "Have you ever known anyone who just, like, understands you completely?"

Larkin wasn't sure she understood herself yet—but she did understand what she was supposed to do, which was nod. No, wait. Shake her head the other way. "No, I guess I haven't. So far I've only dated jerks."

That wasn't precisely true, of course—Larkin could count the number of people she'd dated on three fingers, two of whom she still remembered fondly—but it wasn't supposed to be true. It was supposed to get the truth out of Jessalyn.

"Oh my goodness, me too," Jessalyn said. "I dated so many jerks!" She was using her acting voice again, loud enough to fill the coffee shop, with emphasis standing in for empathy. Larkin would have bet the last few pennies on her credit card that Jessalyn had gone to a high school that staged their annual musical in a cafetorium.

But she chose to place a different bet instead. "Weird question," Larkin said. "Did you ever date Harrison?"

The facade dropped, instantly. Then Jessalyn put it back on, the same way she must have applied the one lipstick in the entire world that didn't stain the rim of a coffee mug. "I'm not going to speak ill of the dead," she said.

"Oh, come on," Larkin said. "The whole point of people being dead is that you can finally talk shit about them."

Jessalyn glanced to either side—no way out, just like Larkin had planned—and then unzipped her purse. "Harrison was just a bad choice," she said, quickly and softly, the tissue already out of her bag. "Everybody makes bad choices sometimes." She patted her nose and eyes. "I'm not going to cry."

"It's okay if you cry." Larkin reached out, put her hand on Jessalyn's soft, round shoulder.

"Well, maybe I don't *want* to cry," Jessalyn said, shaking Larkin's hand away.

When Larkin taught young theater students how to access previously undiscovered emotional depths, she sometimes pulled out this crusty old acting exercise which involved two people saying the exact same sentence, back and forth, until one of them found themselves accessing one of those big emotions—tears, laughter, standing up and throwing their chair across the room. "Maybe you don't want to cry," Larkin repeated, hoping Jessalyn wouldn't respond by tossing a chair.

"I don't want to cry," Jessalyn said, though she was, at this point, technically crying.

"You don't want to cry," Larkin echoed.

"I don't," Jessalyn said, pulling out another tissue. "It was just a bad relationship. I don't even know what happened. I kept telling Harrison I needed to focus on my interviews, and he kept telling me that the academic world was a racket, and then the night before this interview with this job I really wanted, we went to this bar, we were outside on the patio, I was being very careful, and I said I wasn't going to drink anything. Just water. Harrison told me that I should loosen up, that the worst thing about me was that I was a little goody-goody who kept spouting these insipid inspirational phrases—no, he said the worst thing was that I believed them—and then I said I would have one drink, and the next thing I knew, I was in his bed."

Jessalyn had cried through all of the tissues in her little plastic packet. Larkin passed her a napkin. "You were in his bed."

"He was so drunk," Jessalyn said. "Of course he drank constantly, but I'd never seen him like that. He kept saying that he didn't know what to do, and that he was sorry, and that he was trying to help me. And then I fell asleep, for almost the entire day. And then I woke up and got my things and took myself to the hospital."

She took another drink from her coffee cup. This time, the lipstick smeared against the rim. "They told me it was my own sleeping pills, and that there was no sign of. . . anything else. That I should be careful mixing pills and alcohol. That I was lucky."

"You were lucky." Larkin remembered her internet research; it could have gone much worse for Jessalyn. "So you didn't press charges or anything."

"Sometimes the best thing you can do with your life is what *you* want to do with it," Jessalyn said. "I wanted to move on." She looked down at her mug; rubbed at the lipstick stain until it disappeared. "Anyway, I'm not sure there were any charges I could press. I couldn't prove he did anything. Maybe I took the pills myself and forgot about it. I was so stressed out that year."

"It was a stressful year," Larkin said.

"It's better now," Jessalyn said, "but you know what it was like. I didn't know where I'd be living or teaching or working or doing anything."

"Neither did I," Larkin said. "That's why I ended up here."

"I used to think that would be a terrible thing," Jessalyn said. "I was one of those girls that grows up in the middle of nowhere and dreams about getting out of it, you know? But now I'm glad that I get to stay in Iowa." She sipped her coffee again; wiped away the smudge. "I'm also glad Harrison's dead. I hope you don't think I'm a terrible person. The one thought I couldn't get out of my head, all this time, was *what if he does it to someone else?* And then it would be my fault, maybe. Now I don't have to worry about that." She let out a small, sparkling laugh, the way she must have laughed when she played the Fairy Godmother in Rodgers and Hammerstein's *Cinderella*. "I worry about a lot. But having Adam in my life has changed everything, you know? And therapy. Have you done therapy yet?"

"Not really," Larkin said. She'd actually tried therapy once, the first semester she'd failed at completing her dissertation. The campus mental health center had evaluated her and placed her in group therapy, which she left after the third session because everyone else in the group was dealing with the kinds of problems that she, like, directed plays about *for fun*. It also made her less interested in directing anything that dealt with rape or abuse, which was roughly half of the theatrical canon. In some ways those three therapy sessions had set her dissertation progress back another year.

"Well, I recommend it to everybody," Jessalyn said. "And love. I cannot recommend love enough. Once you've got love, it's like the rest of your life falls into place."

"I'll keep that in mind when I send out my CV."

"Oh, that's right," Jessalyn said. "I was going to look at your CV. How about you email it over sometime, and then we can get together again and chat?"

"Sure," Larkin said, even though she had no intention of doing either. She'd already gotten everything that she needed from Jessalyn, and was ready to let her go back to the happiness she had worked so hard to deserve.

CHAPTER 16

Larkin arrived fifteen minutes early to the final dress rehearsal, Ed's YMCA T-shirt laundered and line-dried and smelling vaguely of her mother's eco-friendly detergent. She'd folded it on top of her Beethoven score, carrying it carefully into the orchestra hall and hoping the sweat on her palm wouldn't leave a mark.

Ed was among the people setting up chairs, 150 on risers for the choir plus another 40 in front for the orchestra, and when Larkin waved and said "I brought you your shirt" like an absolute dork, she could have come up with something better than that but apparently she'd wanted to say it as quickly as possible, Ed waved back and said "Thanks!" Then Larkin realized that he wasn't going to say anything else—and that it was a little disappointing, though she didn't know what she'd expected—so she called out "I'll put it on your bag!" and began helping with the chairs and, when that was finished, the music stands.

By then the stage was full of musicians, choristers and orchestrers, and when Larkin went back to her seat in the alto section she saw that Anni was in the seat next to it. Because of course she would be; they didn't need her to play piano anymore. Larkin should have thought of this in advance and come up with a plan, something to say that would fix everything that had gone wrong between them —and then she decided to just tell the truth. "I'm sorry about the other day."

"I know," Anni said. "It's okay, though. I took your advice and pitched the peanut allergy story to my life insurance client. Now I'm going to write it, so nobody can ever say I lied."

"You're writing something about peanut allergies?" It was Marlene, taking the chair on the other side of Anni.

"Yes," Anni said. "Peanut allergies in adults. I thought of it because of Harrison."

"Oh," Marlene said. She sat down; then she stood up again. "I'll be right back."

"You have four minutes," Anni said, and then she turned back to Larkin. "I talked to Sam Nagel again, too. I apologized, and had to listen to him go on about how Millennials were the most unprofessional generation he'd ever seen, but he isn't going to bill me and he did agree to be a source." She smiled. "Lawyers will do anything to improve their SEO."

"Except dig up Harrison's death certificate."

"Right," Anni said. "Maybe it's time to let that go."

"Maybe not," Larkin said. "I've got a bunch of new information. I talked to Shawnta, and I interviewed Jessalyn, and I even started putting together a timeline." Marlene was back, looking a bit like she'd used her four minutes to throw up—no, smelling like it. She looked mostly the same, now that Larkin had taken a minute to pay attention. Graying hair, gripping hands, lips pressed together as she pulled open her purse and offered a packet of gum that both Anni and Larkin refused. Marlene chewed and swallowed her own piece quietly as Maestro Kimbrough took first the stage and then the podium.

"We will begin," he said, and they did.

The dress rehearsal went surprisingly well; Larkin's theater training had led her to expect nothing but disaster on dress rehearsal nights, from costumes splitting their seams to flats toppling over to actors forgetting every line they'd ever learned, but the orchestra was prepared and Maestro Kimbrough was precise and they made it through the entire fourth movement without stopping. Then, of course, there were notes—Larkin thought of Ed, and how he would have made a joke about the word's double meaning—and a second run-through with stops, and then Maestro Kimbrough asked two of the sopranos to switch places because "your section is unbalanced," and they continued until Maestro Kimbrough's phone beeped and it was time for the ten-minute break.

"Anni," Marlene said, as the orchestra members stood and the choral members sat, "do you need a ride to Iowa City on Saturday?"

"Thank you, yes," Anni said. Larkin had not yet thought about how she was going to get to Iowa City for the first of their two performances; she had assumed she would put the address into her phone and then point her car in that direction, but at this point she wasn't sure she could afford the gas. She had driven to rehearsal with her fuel light blinking and hoped to drive back the same way.

So, after Anni and Marlene worked out the details of when Marlene would pick Anni up from her apartment, and after Anni said that she was going to go brave the line for the toilets, Larkin followed her. "Are people, like, carpooling?" she asked, the two of them at the end of a spool of women that stretched ten people beyond the restroom's door. "Is there a signup I could get on?"

"There's no signup," Anni said. "People just offer me rides because I don't have a car." Everyone in the line moved up one person-width. "Do you want to ride with Marlene and me? I'm sure she wouldn't mind."

Larkin didn't really want to ride with grumpy, pukey Marlene, who probably didn't have norovirus since she had made it through the entire rehearsal without running back to the bathroom, but still—well, Larkin just didn't want to catch anything. On the other hand, she couldn't afford not to. "Sure," she said. They all took another big step forward. "Do you want to hear what I learned from Jessalyn?"

"Not here," Anni whispered, conspiratorially. Then, in her normal voice: "But you could come to my apartment before Iowa City if you'd like. We could have lunch. I have apples and cheese and bread and butter. The bread is homemade, the cheese and butter are not."

"What about the apples?" Larkin had missed Anni. She hadn't realized it until that moment, because it was hard to miss someone you hadn't realized was a friend.

"They're from the farmers' market, of course," Anni said, and then she smiled, and then the two of them finally made it into the restroom.

After they got back, and after Anni asked Marlene if Larkin could ride with them to Iowa City—Marlene initially looked as if she wanted to say no, but Iowa Friendly prevailed—the megachoir and the orchestra sat patiently as Ed re-explained the logistics he had already sent in two previous emails. Larkin had gotten into the habit of reading every email Ed sent, including all of the ones she'd ignored the first time. It was the last thing she did before she plugged in her phone and went to sleep.

"Our concert will begin with Samuel Barber's Adagio for Strings, and then we're going to launch right into the Beethoven," Ed said, his anxious energy gone now that he was back on the podium. "No intermission."

"Tell your relatives they must buy their popcorn before the performance," Maestro Kimbrough said. It was almost a joke, or the closest thing the Maestro would ever get to making one.

"The choir will process in between the Barber and the Beethoven," Ed continued. "It's going to be quick and quiet. I'll be backstage to make sure you're all lined up and ready, so pay attention to who's sitting next to you right now because they'll be the people on either side of you when you walk onstage."

"We will practice this," Maestro Kimbrough added.

"Right," Ed said. "Soon as we're done talking through this, we'll have you practice. There will be chairs set up for you, so you can remain seated for the first three movements of the Beethoven. That's going to be an hour of sitting, so be prepared. Use the toilet first, pack your folder full of cough drops and tissues, whatever you need. Yes, you can bring bottles of water with you."

"Plain bottles with no logos, please," Maestro Kimbrough said. "I see someone holding something very neon and green." Anni pressed the stopper back into her bright green bike bottle and shoved it under her chair. "I do not want to buy a new water bottle for this," she whispered to Larkin. "I'll bring one for you," Larkin whispered back. Then she realized she had just volunteered to do something nice for a friend. She couldn't remember the last time she'd done that.

"Soloists, you're going to remain backstage until the break between the third and fourth movements," Ed said. "Then you'll stand in front of the orchestra, downstage right. We'll have the stage marked for you. I'm sure you can handle it, you're all pros."

"Thanks, Ed," said Ben the baritone. "Will we get to see the marks before the show?"

"Of course," Ed smiled. "We're going to make sure everyone has what they need to make this concert a success. And on that note—pun intended—let's have the choir file off the stage so we can practice filing back on." He hopped off the podium and began walking towards the altos. "Larkin, we'll lead the way."

"Okay," Larkin said, her voice loud and overly eager, her face turning unexpectedly warm. It was junior-high level at best, to get excited about standing in line next to the boy you liked—and now she had to admit she liked Ed, she hadn't wanted to, but she did, she liked walking into the dark cinderblock halls with Ed next to her and Anni behind her and the whole choir following them. It felt like—no, it did *not* feel like home.

But there Ed was, telling her how great the choir sounded and how excited he was for the performance, and Larkin felt Ed's excitement as her own, and then Larkin thought of how wonderful it was to know him. Even if he never liked her back. Just to know that a person like Ed existed and would be walking around in the world and doing things. Teaching people. Making art. It made her feel fluttery, and Larkin did not usually think of herself as a fluttery person. She was sad when Ed left, to walk his way back 150 choristers and tell the front of the line to start moving in the other direction, and she blushed again —yes, that was what it was, she was blushing—when she followed the choir back onto the stage and saw that Ed was giving everyone who passed him a high-five. Marlene, stiff and grim; Anni, efficient and precise; and then her hand against his, what should have been a crisp motion turning into a clasp and a squeeze and a "Thanks, Larkin," though Larkin did not know what Ed could possibly be thanking her for, since she had to be one of the least prepared members of the choir. She'd only learned the German inadvertently, and still avoided singing the opening syllables of the words she wasn't quite sure of.

Maybe he was thanking her for existing. Or for bringing back his shirt. Or for not quitting the choir, or for helping him sort music, or taking the check to Anni, or for being there when Harrison died, or for nudging him into talking about tension and release cycles while they waited for the ambulance. Larkin had a whole story with Ed, one she hadn't realized until she told it to herself. But everything in it had happened. Not like the story she had made up about Harrison, both when he was alive and now, about this murder. Which, again, *probably didn't happen.* She should take Anni's advice and let the whole thing go.

But she'd still have lunch with Anni on Saturday, because it would be nice to have lunch with a friend. And she'd bring Anni one of her mother's eco-friendly water bottles. She wouldn't forget. *Water bottle water bottle water bottle*—no, that wasn't the right way to make sure she remembered. They still had several measures and all of Ben's solo before the choir was supposed to sing, so Larkin nudged Anni, whispered "can I borrow your pencil," and when Anni passed it over, wrote "bring Anni water bottle" on the front of her score.

CHAPTER 17

"It's going to be a lovely evening for a party," Josephine said, as she and Larkin pulled plastic wrap off paper plates. "I was afraid it was going to rain."

Larkin had checked the weather app on her phone, though she'd hardly needed to; she'd woken up that morning feeling like a weight had been lifted. Turns out that's what happens when the humidity drops from 98 percent to a mere 73. The air, as she unfolded the legs of her mother's card table and found a level section of backyard on which to set it, felt almost breathable. Chilly, even; or at least cool enough for Larkin to put on the sweater her mother had given her and be glad of it. The endless summer was finally turning into autumn, orange-tinged leaves fluttering from a tree that Larkin had not even realized was there. This might have been the first time she'd actually set foot in her mother's backyard, much less set up a card table. The one time she'd visited for Christmas, instead of demanding her mother come visit her in Los Angeles or New York or wherever she'd been at the time (because academics get paid time off and coffee-slingers/assistant directors/rideshare drivers do not), it had snowed too heavily for her to want to go outside; she'd spent the three days eating Boy Scout popcorn on her mother's sofa and checking her phone to ensure her return flight hadn't been canceled. Now Larkin stood in the cool (though not yet crisp) Iowa air and, without thinking about it, twirled.

"You have a leaf in your hair," Larkin's mother said as soon as Larkin came back inside.

"I know," Larkin said. She twitched her nose at her mother. "Hey, do you mind if I borrow your barrette again?"

"You mean the one you never gave back?" Her mother returned the nose twitch. "It's yours, if you want it. I have plenty."

"I'm not going to keep it forever," Larkin said. She'd looked at herself in the mirror before they began putting the party together: blue jeans, floral blouse, cornflower cardigan. She was as put-together as she needed to be, but she still didn't look like herself. All the clothes that used to look like her were worn out, stained, or otherwise inappropriate for a little get-together to celebrate fall. So she was wearing the clothes she had rarely worn, before. The ones her mother had given her. The ones that made her look like her mother—which was the first thing nearly every party guest said, when they arrived.

"And so tall!" Dr. Something-or-another added, while handing Larkin's mother a gift bag with crumpled tissue paper sticking out of the top. Josephine said "I know!" in a voice that implied it was still a surprise, passing the bag to Larkin so she could put it in the kitchen with the others. Josephine did not say "She gets it from her father," which is what she had always told Larkin, often with a reminder that her height might be her only paternal inheritance. At this party, it was as if Larkin had sprung fully-formed from her mother's head—and not just in terms of her progeneration. Every time Larkin was introduced to one of the guests whom she had invited on her mother's behalf, Josephine added an impressive, preposterously true detail. "Larkin worked on that play with Benedict Cumberbatch —you know, the one that won all the awards." "When she was twelve I used to have her help me grade my papers." "I still have the sonnet Larkin wrote me when she was five years old."

Never mind that Larkin's primary job on that play had been to take both notes and lunch orders; never mind that "grading papers" meant little more than sitting side by side with her mother and passing her a fresh essay when she'd finished marking the previous one; never mind that the sonnet was a four-line poem with a haphazard rhyme scheme and the word "Sonet" written across the top. Larkin's mother was telling the story of her life in a way that made them both sound more accomplished than they actually were, and Larkin let her do it. It was her party, after all.

Which meant that after Larkin had been introduced to everybody, and after she had lined up the gift bags and uncorked the bottles of wine and dumped a second bag of ice into the beer-and-soda cooler, she had nothing to do but stand under the tree and watch. She watched her mother, in the center of the largest cluster of people, tell jokes and laugh at other people's stories and put a comforting hand on a colleague's upper arm. Larkin also watched her mother *pay attention to the details*—making sure there were still enough pretzels in the bowl, making sure the other clusters of people were happily conversing, making sure there wasn't anybody walking up the driveway who needed to be welcomed and brought into the fold.

Because they were both—Larkin and her mother—watching for Claire.

Larkin saw her first; the square silhouette approaching the backyard gate quietly and almost hesitantly, as if Claire was not sure she had arrived at the right home. But Larkin and her mother had spent part of that morning attaching autumn-colored balloons to both the mailbox and the waist-high metal gate, with a third trio of balloons tied to a brick at the edge of the driveway, so it couldn't really be that. It was just—Claire was nervous, that's what she was, and then Larkin was nervous, because that was all her fault, and then her mother saw Claire and she became nervous in the way that only Larkin could tell, and then Larkin's mother apologized to her cluster of guests and Larkin apologized to her mother in her head and both of them went to the gate to meet Claire.

"Hey," Claire said. "Hi." She held up a cardboard carton. "I brought some fizzy water."

"Thank you," Josephine said. "We don't have any of that."

"Nope," Larkin added. "Just plain old boring water. No bubbles."

This was all going very well.

"Here," Josephine continued, "let's let you in. Larkin, can you take the sparkling water?"

"Sure," Larkin said. Claire handed the twelve-pack over the gate as Josephine opened it. The gate wasn't locked or anything; her mother was just being hospitable. Larkin stepped out of the way to let Claire pass through.

"Nice place," Claire said.

"Thank you," Josephine said again. She was flushed; she put one hand up to a reddened cheek and then extended it out to Claire. "Why don't I introduce you to everybody?"

So the three of them went from one cluster of guests to another, Larkin with her arms wrapped around a box of sparkling water, as Josephine explained to everyone that they had met Claire when Larkin had heroically called 911 after finding a man collapsed outside of the orchestra hall. None of what Josephine said was true, though it had all technically happened; in this retelling, Larkin had been brave and Claire had taken care of her, and now Claire was at this party because Larkin had issued the invitation. Of course, anyone who was paying attention to what was actually going on would notice that, after the rounds had been made and the cans of fizzy water unboxed and burrowed into the cooler, Claire remained by Josephine's side and Larkin went right back to her solo spot under the tree.

And then, after the party had gone on long enough that people started putting down their empty beverages and pulling out their phones, Claire joined her.

"Nice party," Claire said, because it had been.

"Thank you for coming."

"Thank you for inviting me." Larkin couldn't tell if Claire's *you* was meant to encompass both herself and her mother, or if Claire was fully aware of how—and why— the invitation had been issued. She suspected the latter; Claire's eyes were twinkling, just a little.

"You know, your mother thinks the world of you," Claire continued. "She told me everything you've done since you've moved here."

"I haven't done much," Larkin said, watching her mother watch them both. "I joined a choir, I screwed up a job interview, I found a dead body." She felt the shame of all the ways she failed Harrison, all over again. "He was dead, wasn't he, when I found him? I keep thinking there was something I could have done to save him." *Like solve his murder.*

"There wasn't anything you could have done," Claire said. "He went into anaphylactic shock and tried to inject himself with epinephrine, but it didn't work. If he'd been able to call 911 right away, we might have been able to do something, but—"

"Harrison didn't carry a phone," Larkin said.

"Yeah, that's what his ex-wife said. And that music conductor." Larkin blushed, slightly, and watched both her mother and Claire notice. "Why isn't he at this party?" Claire asked, her eyes twinkling again.

"My mom's kind of in charge of whether he gets tenure," Larkin said. "It's an academic thing. She's like his boss."

"Ah," Claire said. Then: "I heard you came home one day wearing his shirt."

Now Larkin really was blushing. "I guess my mom really did tell you everything."

"I guess I have you to thank for that," Claire said.

"I guess so," Larkin said, and then she saw her mother wave them both over to another group of people so she could retell the story of how they all met, the no-longer-morbid anecdote of the body and the ambulance and the police station passed along to the few people who didn't yet know how proud and delighted Josephine Day was to have such a daughter and such a new friend.

In the end Claire was the last of the guests to leave, making offers and excuses to help wipe tables and recycle cans. Larkin watched the two of them through the kitchen window, her mother shaking and then holding Claire's hand over the closed gate. It looked like it had been a good idea to send the invitation after all. Larkin had trusted her instincts, and they'd been right—at least in this case.

She wasn't so sure about the other case she was currently working on.

CHAPTER 18

"But that doesn't make sense," Anni said, filling the water bottle Larkin had brought her. "I mean, it does, epinephrine injectors are fiddly and you have to get it right when you're actively dying, but. . . he'd done it before." She put down the bottle and picked up her mug of tea. "That one time he ate a wrong cookie. He pulled the thing out of his bag, jabbed himself in the leg, and then he went to the hospital."

"How much was he drinking then?" Larkin sat on Anni's sofa with her own mug of tea—spearmint this time, a choice she was already regretting—and scootched over to give Anni room to join her. They were both dressed in black, in preparation for that afternoon's concert; Larkin was wearing the same dress she had worn to Harrison's funeral.

"I don't know," Anni said. "I suppose not as much as he was now. You couldn't really start smelling it on him until this summer."

Larkin tried to remember if she'd ever smelled alcohol on Harrison. She'd only really had conversations with him outside, and she mostly remembered smelling humidity. Today was also unexpectedly, unseasonably humid; the sky was gray and slashed through with black clouds, as if it were going to perform the Beethoven that afternoon as well.

"Which means he probably started drinking more after Jessalyn was drugged," Larkin said. "Because everyone thought he did it."

"Do you think he did it?"

"No." It was a trust-your-instincts thing, again. "But everyone else did, and according to Shawnta something happened at that soloist rehearsal that made Harrison feel extra terrible, and then we had the rehearsal where Jessalyn cried, and then. . ." There was an alternative to murder that Larkin hadn't considered until that moment. "Do you think he killed himself?"

"Because he couldn't handle the stress of being wrongly accused?"

"Maybe," Larkin said. "Let's say he was drinking too much, he couldn't take it anymore, he decides to grab something off the snack table, he goes outside to eat it, his airways start closing up, he changes his mind, he tries to inject himself, but it's too late." She took another sip of her toothpaste-flavored tea. "Or maybe it wasn't like, suicide-suicide. Maybe he just wants to go to the hospital so he doesn't have to play any more of the rehearsals, but he screws up the injector because he's drunk."

"Nobody wants to go to the hospital," Anni said. "And nobody wants to go into anaphylactic shock on purpose."

"So it was either a tragic accident or suicide, then."

"I don't know," Anni said. "Something's not right about this."

"That's what I've been saying all along."

Anni stood up, exchanged her cup of tea for a tiny

brass-handled watering can, and began to address her plants. "My rubber tree was down to four leaves, the first winter I had it," she said. "I kept telling it that if it died on me, I'd replace it with a pink cactus—but then it lived, and I just got a pink cactus anyway." She gestured to a cactus that Larkin would have described as green, except for the tips. "But I looked everything up, you know, online. About how to keep rubber plants from losing their leaves." She turned back to Larkin. "It wasn't a tree then. Just maybe a foot high." She turned away again and began watering the succulents lined up on the windowsill. "The internet kept saying that you shouldn't overwater rubber plants. That they only needed watering once a month in winter. Except I finally realized they weren't considering Iowa winters. It gets so dry in here, probably because of all the exposed brick, that I need to water my plants more often, not less." Larkin watched Anni look back at her rubber tree, which was nearly as tall as her plug-in piano. "So I saved it. By doing the opposite of what the internet said."

Larkin didn't know how to respond to this. "Are you comparing Harrison's death to your rubber plant?"

"Of course not," Anni said. "I was making small talk, because we still have five minutes before Marlene is supposed to get here. I'm very bad at small talk. Plants may be too big of a topic." She put the watering can back on the counter and picked up and then sipped her tea. "It's gone cold again."

"That's how entropy works."

"See, this is why I like you." Anni smiled. "I was also thinking that there might be a comparison between the way I thought about my rubber plant and the way we're all thinking about how epinephrine injectors work. Because you and I, we only know those from the internet, right? I've never used one. I've interviewed someone who's used one, for my story, but I've never held one. Maybe something went wrong when Harrison tried to inject himself."

"Maybe the wet air made his leg slippery," Larkin said.

"More likely his hands," Anni said. "I could look into what happens to sweat when your airways close." She tried sipping her tea again, and then put the cup into the sink. "But whatever went wrong still doesn't necessarily mean he was murdered. It could still just be a tragic accident."

"That's what Claire and everyone else seems to think."

"Then maybe that's what we should think too," Anni said. She glanced at her phone. "Also, our ride's here."

———

Larkin felt the first thick, warm raindrop ooze against her arm as she opened the back door of Marlene's car. The second one hit Marlene's windshield as Larkin fastened her seatbelt. Anni was in front, trying the small talk thing with Marlene, who, after asking Anni to help her check to see if it was safe to pull out of the parking space, seemed uninterested in conversation.

But Anni strung words together for a living, and so she continued. "Larkin brought me a plain gray aluminum bottle so I won't have to use my bike bottle, although I rarely end up drinking water during performances because I'm always afraid I'll have to use the bathroom. It's difficult to activate your diaphragm effectively with a full bladder!"

"I'm more concerned that I'll spill water down the front of my dress," Larkin said, trying to help Anni out and keep the conversation from becoming a monologue.

"Those reusable bottles may be good for the environment, but they are hard to drink out of."

"Have you ever noticed how, when you fill an aluminum bottle with water, the sound of the water entering the bottle makes a chromatic scale?" Anni asked, turning in her seat to look at Larkin. "I know that modality is a cultural construction, but it is fascinating to think of the ways in which music and nature intersect." She turned back to Marlene, to try to include her in the conversation once again. "Plus, when you hear the end of the scale you know the bottle's full."

"Huh," Marlene said. She turned on her windshield wipers and pulled onto the highway.

"Wow, it's really starting to rain," Larkin said, and then nobody said anything, and then Marlene clicked the knob that made the windshield wipers go faster.

"I'm working on a story about peanut allergies in adults," Anni said, finally. "Because of Harrison."

Larkin felt the entire car shift and then swerve back into the center of the lane. "Is that how it happened?" Marlene asked. "They know it for sure?"

"Yes," Anni said, quick and precise. "Larkin talked to a police officer about it. Anaphylactic shock."

"Damn," Marlene said, just to herself, and then the car began to speed up. There weren't a lot of other drivers on the highway, but there was a lot of rain, and Larkin reflexively gripped the backseat door handle. "This isn't another derecho, right?" Larkin asked. She hadn't been in Iowa during the last one, but she had read about it. Trees ripped out by the roots; cars blown from their parking spots into the middle of the street.

"Just an ordinary storm," Marlene said, directing her voice towards the backseat. "We get 'em all the time."

She kept driving.

Then she spoke again.

"I shouldn't have done it." That was maybe directed towards Anni; it was hard to tell. Larkin was on the driver's side, so she couldn't see Marlene's face; she saw Anni turn quickly towards her, the same idea occurring to both of them two minutes too late.

"Done what?" Anni said, folding her hands tightly in her lap and keeping her voice chipper and cheerful.

"I wanted him gone," Marlene said. The car shifted into another, faster gear; the water blurred the windows so Larkin couldn't see how close they were to any potential impacts. "Harrison was a shallow, callous man who didn't care who he hurt. He ruined Jessalyn's life."

"I talked to Jessalyn," Larkin said. "Just this week." Larkin didn't know if reassuring Marlene would somehow save them all from skidding or slamming or whatever Marlene planned to do with her rapidly moving vehicle, but it was the only thing she could think of. "Jessalyn's happy. She's engaged to a farmer. She's going to be fine."

"Jessalyn and Adam got engaged?" Anni asked. "Did you see it online? I only check social media once a day and I miss a lot of stuff. You'd think the algorithm would have put the engagement post on the top."

Larkin couldn't tell if Anni was playing along or if this was simply *how she talked, all the time, even when they were in a highly dangerous situation with a potential murderer*—but she was grateful for it, either way. "Jessalyn told me when we met for coffee. I saw the ring."

"Oh wow," Anni said. "Was it huge?"

Larkin couldn't have remembered what Jessalyn's ring looked like even if she had paid attention when she saw it. "It's tasteful."

"Good for her," Marlene said, shutting down the

conversation that Larkin had hoped would slow down the car. "I didn't get an Adam. I got pregnant."

Larkin could see the edges of Marlene's hair poking out on either side of the driver's side headrest. Gray, of course; it had always been gray. But it was also soft, not stiff and sprayed like some of the older women wore theirs, and the one hand Larkin could see, wrapped tightly around the right side of the steering wheel, was smooth, not spotted. Larkin had automatically classified Marlene as "old," thanks to her hair and the way she clutched her purse, but she was probably only in her 50s. About the same age as Larkin's mother.

And Harrison. Women always looked older when they stood next to men who were the same age, while men reflected the youthful glow of the women they ended up dating. That was why everyone assumed that the man and woman in *American Gothic* were a couple, and why Larkin hadn't assumed that Marlene and Harrison had ever been one.

"I'm sorry," Anni said. "Did Harrison know?"

"He drove me to the clinic," Marlene said. "Took off his letter jacket and put it over my head as we walked in, so I wouldn't have to see the people with the signs."

"So you were in high school," Larkin said.

"We both were," Marlene said. "And I got in so much trouble when we got back. My parents assumed Harrison and I had gone off together to have sex—and I let them believe that because I didn't want to tell them what we had really done—so they made me quit the basketball team and the choir. I went straight home after school for the rest of that year. Sat in my room and cried." She sighed, the edge of a sob in the back of her throat. "Of course the rumors got out and nobody would have anything to do with me, so maybe it was better in the end."

Marlene took her right hand off the wheel and swiped it across her face. "I could have gotten scholarships, probably. I was smart, though I was also fool enough to fall for Harrison's charms. But I didn't go to college, not until years later when I got my associate's degree. Harrison went, and I paid attention to every story they told about him, and all of the stories were the same."

The car had started to slow down; Larkin let go of the door handle and exhaled. "I'm so sorry," Anni said again.

"He'd go after anyone who would have him, women, men, it didn't matter," Marlene said. "When he got married I knew it wouldn't last five years." She sniffed; Anni pulled open her backpack and passed over a tissue. "Then I heard what he did to Jessalyn, and how it cost her that job, and how she couldn't even sing in front of him."

The car was now going maybe a little too slow. "Do you think you want to pull over?" Larkin asked, instantly regretting that she hadn't tried to phrase it in a way that would be more likely to achieve its objective.

"No," Marlene said, sobbing. "I have to drive you girls to the concert, and then I have to go to the police, because I killed him." Her angered, anguished wail filled the entire car. "And now everyone's going to find out."

"Pull over first," Larkin said. "It's not safe to be driving like this, and"—Larkin asked herself what she thought Marlene wanted most—"you don't want us to get killed either."

That worked. The car stopped, on the shoulder; Anni stroked Marlene's shoulder awkwardly before handing her the whole packet of tissues. The rain beat against the roof and poured in sheets over the windows.

"I just wanted him to have to quit the rehearsals,"

Marlene said, in between gulps and gasps and sobs. "Like he did when we were singing the Mass in G."

"Because he ate that cookie," Anni said.

"So I thought I'd give him something with peanuts in it, and then he'd get sick, and then Jessalyn wouldn't have to sing in front of him."

"Wow," Larkin said. She hadn't even considered Marlene as a suspect. She was the worst amateur detective ever.

"Except I chickened out," Marlene continued. "I was going to offer Harrison a scotcheroo with peanut butter in it, you couldn't tell, it looked exactly the same, and then. . . well, I couldn't do it."

"Then you couldn't have killed him," Anni said.

"But I didn't label the scotcheroos!" Marlene wailed. "Because I didn't want him to know he was getting a peanut butter one!" She was crying so hard she could hardly breathe. "So I must. . . have put the wrong ones. . . on the wrong tables. . ."

"Oh," Anni said. "But—"

"But you didn't mean to do it." Larkin interrupted Anni, because the next action in the scene was to convince Marlene to calm down. "You're not a murderer." Of course, the objective behind the action was to convince herself that she wasn't the worst amateur detective ever. If Marlene didn't actually do it, then Larkin hadn't failed and none of them would die halfway to Iowa City in a rainstorm.

"I had the motive," Marlene sobbed. "And I baked the weapon."

"*Mens rea* and *actus reus*," Anni said, helpful to the end —which might come sooner than they'd hoped.

"But you never meant to kill him. You only wanted to send him to the hospital for a few days." Larkin could not believe she was making a case for that being *okay*, some-how. "And then you decided not to do it. You didn't actu-ally do anything wrong."

"But he died anyway," Marlene sobbed, blowing her nose loudly into one of Anni's tissues. "And now he's going to ruin my life again, from beyond the grave."

"Well," Anni said, "I suppose you ruined his."

It was a joke, an inadvertent, ridiculous joke, and Larkin had just enough time to say "Anni, what?!" before Anni said "I forgot, you said we could make jokes!" and Marlene said "That was a joke?" and Anni said "I'm sorry, I'm so bad at all of this. We've never done this before! None of us, in this car, has ever done anything like this before!"

Unbelievably, Marlene started the car, the noise just audible above the pounding rain. Larkin and Anni glanced at each other; then Anni pressed the back of her head against the car headrest and gripped the sides of the seat cushions. They were going to die in this car or live long enough to laugh at it all later, that was for sure. Or maybe somewhere in between. There was a lot of in-between in terms of car accidents; Larkin remembered all of the crushed bumpers she had passed on the Los Angeles high-ways. She wished there was something she could do to keep them from ending up in a similar situation. What was it Marlene needed right now? What kind of help could Larkin give?

"Larkin," Marlene said, "can you look out the back to make sure no one's coming?"

Larkin twisted around. All she could see was rain, but she couldn't see headlights. "It's safe," she said, hoping she was right.

Marlene pulled off the shoulder and back onto the highway, quickly getting the little car up to what anyone would consider a reasonable, prudent speed, especially considering the weather. "I'm going to drop you girls off in Iowa City," she said, her voice calm and firm and determined. "Then I'm going to turn around and turn myself in."

"You don't have to do that," Larkin said, although she wasn't actually sure whether that was true. If you believed you played a role in someone's death, accidentally or otherwise, were you required to tell the police? She could ask Anni, although it wasn't really the time or place for it.

"Harrison and I have been lying about our lives since we were young," Marlene said. She took the last tissue out of Anni's packet. "Now I'll go tell them all the truth." Marlene blew her nose one-handedly. "But I'll drop you off first."

"Thanks," Anni said, because one of them had to say something.

Unbelievably, they made it to the Iowa City auditorium with time to spare; unbelievably, Larkin explained to Maestro Kimbrough that Marlene was not feeling well and would not be joining the choir that evening.

"And that's not a lie," she told Anni, as they stood backstage with the rest of the altos—though she was glad she'd only had to tell it to the Maestro and not to Ed, who was currently saying hello to every individual member of the megachoir while wearing an extraordinarily dapper suit. With suspenders. Larkin did not realize how much she loved suspenders until that very moment.

And then there he was, thanking Anni for playing those rehearsals and thanking Larkin for sticking with the choir, adding "I heard about Marlene" in a way that made Larkin wonder how he knew, until she realized he thought Marlene was out sick.

"Here I was hoping she'd bring her famous scotcheroos," Ed joked. "The best in town."

"Yes," Anni said, poker-stiff and completely un-poker-faced. "Very."

"Hey," Ed continued, "if you all aren't doing anything afterwards, a bunch of us are getting together for drinks." He invited them both while looking mostly at Larkin. "You should come."

"Sure," Larkin said, and Ed smiled, and Larkin stage-faked a smile until he was gone, and then she turned to Anni and said "Should we still be doing this concert? Do we need to go to the police station too? Are we, like, accessories to the crime now?"

"If anything, we're accessories to the confession," Anni said, "though I don't know much about the legality of the whole thing. If Marlene is smart, though I suspect she's thinking more with her emotions than with her brain right now, she won't get anything worse than involuntary manslaughter."

"Which is still pretty bad!"

"They might consider the whole thing a horrible accident," Anni continued. "Since Marlene never intended to kill Harrison and she didn't even really intend to poison him. She just thought about it, and how she'd do it, and she came up with the easy, obvious answer. Just like I told you."

"Told me what?"

"I told you that if someone wanted to hurt Harrison they'd make him eat something with peanuts in it," Anni said. "The first night you came to my apartment. I was wearing my skeleton pajamas. You drank cinnamon tea and told me you suspected me of murder."

"Right."

"And now we've solved the murder mystery, I guess,"

Anni said. They were lining up now, preparing to process onstage. "But—"

"Shhh," someone said, because someone always shushed people backstage.

"I'm not sure we should get much credit," Larkin said, more quietly. "Marlene basically told us everything." Something was still bugging Larkin about all of this. "It's like. . . the scene at the end of the movie, where the villain gives a big speech about their evil plans." The stage manager opened the door that connected the auditorium proper to the hallway they were currently standing in; Larkin could hear the audience applauding the orchestra's first piece, the one that always made her think of old war movies. She couldn't remember what it was called. Once again, she hadn't paid attention.

"Except the speech is usually about world domination, not two high schoolers getting an abortion."

"Yeah." They began moving forward. "I feel really bad for Marlene."

"Me too."

———

The performance was uneventful, in the sense that nothing happened that wasn't supposed to happen. The orchestra played the first three movements; the soloists entered; the audience began to applaud and Maestro Kimbrough gave a quick glare that silenced the entire house. The choir stood and sang about friendship or joy or whatever the ode was actually about. Not truth and beauty, this time around. Larkin and Anni had learned the truth, and it was not beautiful.

CHAPTER 19

Ed waved them over the minute they walked into the brewpub, which was how Larkin and Anni ended up squished between Ed and the four soloists at the far end of the bar. Larkin and Ed were the only ones still in concert attire, though Ed's suit and suspenders were by far better looking than Larkin's stretched-out, underarm-stained LBD. Anni had hidden the same outfit she always wore inside the canvas bag she always carried, and changed in the hallway where they had lined up; the soloists had ditched their tails and sequins somewhere between the theater and the pub, and now the four of them shared three barstools.

"I got the bartender to make a special drink for us," Shawnta shouted at Anni and Larkin, holding up a martini glass filled with something purple and a twist. "Ask for the Ode to Joy."

"It's not that good," Ed whispered, each word close enough to brush Larkin's cheek. "Here, try mine. I think it's got grapefruit in it."

"Nobody finds grapefruit joyful," Larkin whispered

back, before carefully lifting and sipping from the drink Ed offered. Martini glasses were inherently unstable, and she did not want to repeat the experience of spilling all over herself. "Wow, that's bad."

"Anni, do you want to try it?" Ed asked. "I could save you ten bucks."

"I don't share drinks," Anni said. She leaned into the bar, her tiny figure somehow commanding enough to get the bartender's attention. "Could I please get a club soda or sparkling water?" She dug into her bag and pulled out a five dollar bill. "You can keep the change."

"Water's free," the bartender said, holding a nozzle over a tumbler. "Perk of being the DD," he added, passing the glass to Anni.

"Oh, I don't drive," Anni said, putting the $5 on the bar and pushing it in the bartender's direction. "I just don't drink. I mean alcohol."

"I don't drink either," Jessalyn said, to Anni, the bartender, the world. "Not anymore." She sucked at her soda straw and swiveled around on her stool, her eyes scanning the door, the crowd, the door again—"Adam!"— and she hopped down and was gone.

"You should grab that seat," Ed said, even though both of them were standing; Larkin took it, putting herself between Gerald and the seat Ben and Shawnta were currently sharing. Then she scanned the cocktails chalked above the bar, ordered something called the Crunchberry (when in Iowa, after all), and when the bartender passed her a martini glass filled with something pink and rimmed with both sugar and cereal bits, she realized uncomfortably that she probably didn't have enough money to pay for it.

"You didn't want the Ode to Joy?" Shawnta asked.

"I can't do grapefruit," Larkin said. It hurt her sweet tooth.

"Medication thing?" Ben asked, though he didn't pause long enough for Larkin to answer. "Do you remember the last time we were all here? Gerald, wasn't it right after you got back from that thing in Baja California?"

"Yes," Gerald said, his back to the bar, one hand wrapped around a beer bottle.

"He got into this vocal intensive program," Shawnta explained to Larkin. "Big deal."

"Right," Larkin said. She'd participated in a few artistic intensives of her own; the kind of thing where anyone who could afford $5 grand and a week off from work could spend it studying with some of the bigger (though never the biggest) names in the business. Those kinds of things never helped your resume as much as you thought they would, but they were conveniently tax-deductible, and the better intensives put you up in a fancy hotel and gave you enough time to explore whatever scenic locale you were coincidentally visiting.

"Wasn't Harrison there that night, too?" Ben continued. "God bless him. I remember the two of you were standing six feet apart. Well, Gerald, at least you won't have to worry about *that* anymore."

Larkin watched Gerald stiffen, then slowly raise his bottle to his lips. He was trying to look like he didn't care about whatever Ben was referring to—and when he failed to pull it off, he walked away.

"Straight boys are so sensitive," Ben said. He turned to Shawnta. "Should we tell him we know he's not gay? Like, absolutely *never ever*, one hundred percent *not gay*?"

"Gerald can go piss himself," Shawnta said. She twisted one shoulder around; waved at the bartender. "I would love another Ode to Joy when you get a minute. Thank you!"

"I cannot believe you're drinking those," Ben said.

"Right?" Larkin said again, feeling like she ought to participate in the conversation—though it was probably a bad idea to comment on someone else's drink while holding a martini glass with breakfast cereal crushed against the rim.

"Kel always makes me something special, after every performance," Shawnta said. "Wait! That wasn't the last time we were here! It was at the end of this summer, after we did all of those chamber gigs in the park. Songs from Shakespeare! We were all outside, they had set up all of those tables on the sidewalk, Kel made those vodka martinis with the pickle spears in them!"

"Was that what made Jessalyn so sick?" Ben said. "I'm sorry, I'm terrible. Didn't she get wasted that night, though?"

Larkin saw Shawnta glance at her—a reflexive woman-to-woman look—and then lie to Ben. "Yeah. Harrison took her home."

Which meant Shawnta knew, and didn't think Harrison had done it either. Larkin swallowed a mouthful of pink drink, hoping it would loosen up her brain enough for her to come up with a way to ask Shawnta about this without getting Ben involved—the tampon thing, she should get Shawnta to go to the bathroom with her and then ask for a tampon, but she wouldn't even need to do that, she'd just need to get Shawnta into the bathroom with her somehow—but Larkin's brain clamped down around the impulse. *Let it go,* Larkin told herself. *You've already done enough.*

Then she felt a familiar hand on her shoulder. It was Ed, she knew it, without even having to turn around—and knowing it made her flinch just enough to slop alcohol out of her martini glass and onto her dress.

"Hey," Ed said. "Do you need a ride back? I'm taking Anni. She was going to take the bus."

"I still could take the bus," Anni said. "It's no big deal. I take it all the time."

"Consider it my treat, to thank you for all that extra work you did for us."

"Would you mind taking Larkin, too?" Anni asked. "She and I came over here together, and her car's at my apartment."

Ed didn't ask Larkin why her car was at Anni's apartment instead of, like, parked outside the bar, but Larkin felt like she ought to provide an answer anyway. "Because we took the bus. Because I can't afford to buy gas right now." She laughed, and tried to avoid Anni's eyes. "In fact, this drink is probably the last thing I'll be able to buy for a while. Good thing I'm a thirty-five-year-old adult who lives with her mother, right?"

Then she tried to avoid Ed's eyes, and ended up staring at the few bits of crumbled cereal left on the rim of her glass. "I'll grab the drink," Ed said. "You can treat me when things get better."

So Ed paid, and then they left the bar and Anni—who had not said anything to Larkin since the lie about how they got to Iowa City—took the front seat in Ed's car. Larkin listened to the two of them make Anni's version of small talk, which in this case meant discussing the comparative acoustics of their various performance and rehearsal spaces, and then she said, "Ed, we didn't take the bus over here. I don't know why I told you that, because it wasn't true. We rode with Marlene."

"I thought she was sick," Ed said.

"See, that wasn't true either," Larkin said.

"I don't know how much we can say," Anni quickly added, turning her head to catch Larkin's eyes. Larkin nodded. "There was an emergency," she explained, hoping that would be honest enough for both Ed and Anni. "A personal one. Marlene dropped us off and went back to CR."

"I'm sorry to hear that," Ed said. "I hope she's okay."

"Yeah," Larkin said. "Me too."

They were silent for a moment. Then Anni turned around again. "There's nothing wrong with living with your mother when you're an adult," she said. "Parents, family—they help you out."

"That's not what my namesake said," Larkin said, a joke she wasn't sure anyone in the car would get. She thought about her father, who would have gotten it, and then decided to think about him later.

"And your mom likes you," Ed said. "She asks me about you whenever I see her."

"I know," Larkin said. "It's fine. It's all fine. It'll all be okay." She realized that now that the mystery was over—now that she and Anni would no longer be pretending to be amateur detectives—that she would have to finish her dissertation and find a job. Maybe she'd have to find a job without finishing her dissertation. Neither option seemed exactly like what she wanted.

But there they were, at Anni's apartment, with her car and its nearly empty gas tank waiting for her—and a goodbye to Ed, and another to Anni, and Anni's response that they'd all see each other again in less than twelve hours, and the realization that as soon as tomorrow's concert was over, then everything would be over and she'd be back where she was at the beginning of the summer.

CHAPTER 20

"You look lovely today," Larkin told her mother, as they stood side-by-side putting coffee into filters and bread into toaster slots.

"I'm your beautiful and well-preserved mother," Josephine said. "Shouldn't you tell me I look lovely every day?"

"Sure," Larkin said, opening the refrigerator and passing her mother the checker-topped jar of jam. "But you look exceptionally lovely today."

"Really?" Josephine asked, one hand going to her hair, which she had not pulled back into its usual barrette. "I mean, I tried. Do you think she'll be able to tell that I tried?"

"Who?"

"Don't tell me you weren't paying attention."

Larkin twitched her nose at her mother. "Oh, you mean Officer Novak."

Her mother twitched her nose back. "Claire and I are going to your concert this evening."

"Like, on a date?"

"Like, maybe?" Josephine mimicked Larkin's incredulity—though Larkin suspected her mother of being a little incredulous about the whole thing herself. "There will be dinner, first, and then Barber and Beethoven and Schiller."

"Who's Schiller?"

Josephine handed Larkin a cup of coffee. "Schiller wrote the ode."

"What, you mean. . . the lyrics?"

Larkin's mother held her own cup of coffee close to her chest and laughed. "It was a poem first. A very famous one. Beethoven wasn't the only composer to set it to music."

"Did you know that before you looked it up online?"

"My darling daughter," Josephine said, and then she began reciting, in her poetry voice:

Wem der grosse Wurf gelungen,
Eines Freundes Freund zu sein,
Wer ein holdes Weib errungen,
Mische seinen Jubel ein!

"I always liked that part of the ode best," she explained, blushing slightly.

"Okay," Larkin said. "If you promise not to laugh at me for not doing my research, or paying attention, or anything like that, will you tell me what it means? Because I know we're not actually singing about Freud."

"Well, there's *Freude*, which means joy, and *Freund*, which means friend. The poem's actually about the joy you find in friendship, and then there's this bit at the end about how friendship proves the existence of God, but you can take or leave that part."

After Larkin's mother sat down with her toast and her laptop, Larkin looked up the Schiller on her phone. Her mother's favorite part of the ode translated, roughly, as follows:

If you've had the great success
Of learning how to be a friend to a friend
If you've done the hard work of creating a loving relationship
Add your joy to ours!

Larkin had not thought of the concept of friendship as something that you could be successful at, before. She had assumed friendship just happened—and if it didn't happen to you, it meant that there was either something wrong with you or, more optimistically, you hadn't found your people yet. Larkin had not expected to find her people in Iowa, and had actively avoided looking for them —but it turns out that she had more success making friends in Pratincola than she had anywhere else in her life. There was a text from Anni on her phone, inviting her to meet "my sister and her accident-prone twins" after the concert. There was also a text from Ed—Larkin had never gotten a text from Ed before—asking Larkin if she wouldn't mind doing something with him while the rest of the choir was gathering in the green room.

Larkin texted *sure what* and then wondered if Ed was the kind of guy who preferred his texts with punctuation attached.

The response came almost immediately.

meet me at the spot where Harrison died

———

Larkin wondered what Ed would think when she pulled up to the stage door on her mother's old ten-speed, wearing her mother's old bike helmet. He appeared to approve—at least, he was smiling. His smile got wider when Larkin took off the bike helmet and made a show of shaking out her long, dark hair.

"I see you've decided to join the Cycle Club," Ed said.

"Not yet," Larkin said. "I can't afford the dues." She was wearing her favorite jeans, her favorite T-shirt, and her favorite hoodie; her concert dress, choir folder, and water bottle were all tucked inside the backpack she had used in high school. Back then, she had worn it over one shoulder; now it was secured on both sides, and Larkin found herself fiddling with the straps. Not because she was nervous, of course. There was no reason to be nervous. She was just—here, with Ed, on the steps where Harrison had died. Where he injected himself with epinephrine and waited to be able to breathe. Where she found his body, and where the two of them waited, together, until the police arrived.

"Sorry," Larkin said. "This is weird."

"I know," Ed said. "It might have been a bad idea. I just felt like you and I ought to do something, because nobody else is going to do anything for Harrison tonight. I managed to convince the board that we should have *in memory of* in the program, but they stuck it on the penulti-mate page, in the middle of a bunch of ads."

He opened his suit jacket—suspenders, again—and took the program out of an inside pocket. "See? Nobody's going to flip that far through. I wanted them to put it in the front, a full page with photograph, but they wouldn't do it."

"Because of the rumors," Larkin said.

Ed looked at Larkin—not a sidelong glance, but a proper eyes-meeting look. "I know I'm not supposed to say this," he said, "but I don't believe he did it."

"Neither do I," Larkin said.

"I didn't know what to do," Ed said. "Do I tell him he

can't play? Do I tell Jessalyn she can't sing? And then he up and dies, which solves both problems at once."

Larkin looked carefully at Ed, but pulled her gaze away before he could look back. He still thought Harrison had died accidentally. It may still have been an accident, depending on what the police decided to do with Marlene's confession—and Larkin decided to trust Ed enough to tell him everything she knew.

"I know I'm not supposed to say this," Larkin said, "but—"

Ed's phone beeped; he glanced down, and his entire face shifted into delight. "My parents just got here," he said. "Drove all the way from St. Louis, even though I won't even be onstage for this one. I'm going to go show them to their seats, and then it'll be time to warm up the choir. See you in the rehearsal room?"

"Of course," Larkin said.

Ed smiled, lifted his right hand slightly, second-guessed it, second-guessed the second-guessing, and then let his hand travel all the way to Larkin's shoulder. A touch, a squeeze, a quick removal to his pocket.

"Say goodbye to Harrison for me, okay?" Ed said.

Larkin nodded. "I will."

She watched the door close behind him.

Then she watched it open again.

"Are you Larkin Day?"

The question came from a woman Larkin almost recognized: slight, wearing a black cardigan and holding a leather satchel. Anni held the stage door for her; the two of them joined Larkin on the back steps.

"This is she," Larkin said, defaulting to the phone etiquette her mother had taught her back when phones didn't immediately identify callers, the back of her mind pulling up the first polite response it ever learned because the front of her mind had recognized the satchel, if not the person carrying it. "That's Harrison's bag," she said, less politely.

"Yes," the woman said, her eyes glancing between Anni and Larkin and the ground. "They gave it to his grandmother, because she was next of kin. I thought you might want to have it."

That was why Larkin should have recognized the woman—she had been behind Harrison's grandmother at the funeral, pushing the wheelchair. Same cardigan, different shoes. No mask, this time. A face, soft and shy.

"There's a note in it, for you," the woman continued. "That's why I thought you should have the bag."

"The whole bag?" That was from Anni.

"His grandmother doesn't want it," the woman said. "She told me to throw it away. It's good leather."

The woman was wearing cheap, plastic ballet flats that had started to crack at the seams. She could have kept the bag for herself, or sold it. "Thank you," Larkin said. "You didn't have to do that."

"I just figured," the woman said. "After I read the note." She held the well-worn satchel out to Larkin. "I'm sorry, I probably shouldn't have. But it wasn't in an envelope or anything. It was just in there."

"That's okay," Larkin said, her polite brain once again taking over. She took the satchel, Anni held the door again, and the woman went back into the orchestra hall. "Enjoy the concert," Larkin said, a few seconds too late, one hand already digging into Harrison's bag.

The note was not difficult to find. Harrison's grandmother's nurse had, presumably, removed Harrison's wallet and keys; all that was left was a battered spiral notebook, a scattering of pencils, a full packet of tissues, an empty packet of cigarettes, and Harrison's flask. The note itself had been torn out of the notebook and folded in half, with the words "Larkin Day" written in pencil on the outside fold.

Larkin hoisted the bag over her shoulder, feeling it slap against her backpack. Then she read what Harrison had written on the inside of the paper, first to herself and then to Anni.

Dear Larkin,

I am sorry that I did not call you this week as promised. I find myself a bit gun-shy, which is unusual for me. If you've heard any of the gossip about my personal life, you know that I have a reputation as a bit of a Lothario. (I write that not knowing who Lothario actually was. Part of me imagines that you must know, you're clever enough, and you'll tell me all about him when we finally have our drink together.)

Of course, if you've heard any of the gossip about my personal life, you've also heard what I've been accused of doing. I want to assure you that none of it is true, but I find myself wanting to avoid the conversation even more. I suppose that is why I have chosen to write you instead of speak over the phone, or arrange a time in which we can speak in person.

And yet I already regret what might have been, between us. You are exactly the kind of woman I cannot help but be attracted to. I have always had a soft spot for the temporarily lost, perhaps because I have so often turned down the opportunity to be found.

We could have romped, and parted, and you would have been stronger for it. And yet the weakness of one woman has made me worry that it will never be like that again—and so I have chosen weakness myself, and have not initiated this possibility.

Forgive me.

Harrison

"What a fucking asshole," Anni said.

"I don't know," Larkin said. Her eyes were still stuck on the bottom third of the letter; the one where he described Larkin as "temporarily lost" and Jessalyn as "weak." She decided Anni was right. "No, I agree. What a fucking asshole."

"What a fart-snuggling presumptuous shih tzu dog," Anni said, and then Larkin said "Oh, is that what you meant to say the first time?" and the two of them started laughing, Harrison's bag around Larkin's shoulder and his letter half-crumpled in her hand. "We could have romped, and parted, and you would have been stronger for it," Larkin said, in her most pompous, dramatic, theater-trained voice, and Anni laughed so hard she snorted.

"I cannot believe he wrote that," Larkin said.

"I can," Anni said. "And it's so obvious that he wants you to read it and take pity on him and go to bed with him anyway."

"I might have done it," Larkin said.

"Then it's probably a very good thing that he's dead," Anni said. "Since I'm pretty sure you're not the necrophiliac type."

"Nope," Larkin said. "I prefer the living." She pulled Harrison's flask out of his bag and raised it into the air. "To men who are alive, and who are not jerks!"

"Who know how to play the piano like an accompanist, not a soloist," Anni added.

"Who own smartphones!" Larkin continued. "Why didn't he own a smartphone?"

"He could have used it to look up who Lothario was!" Anni said, still laughing. "He would have made you tell him. He would have made you set up all the dates, and he probably would have made you pay for everything."

"He would have been out of luck there," Larkin said. "I couldn't have bought him a drink if I'd wanted to."

"Well," Anni said, "it's a good thing he always carried his own."

Larkin looked at the flask she was holding and thought of Harrison as she had known him. A player, in every sense of the word—but also a thoughtful, kind, potentially decent man. Any judgment on his life wasn't hers to pass.

"To Harrison," Larkin said, softly this time. "We should do this the right way," she told Anni, as she unscrewed the cap on the flask. "Let's drink to Harrison, and then go find the rest of the choir."

"I don't share drinks," Anni said. "And you shouldn't either. Harrison's germs have had plenty of time to reproduce in there."

"The alcohol probably killed them all," Larkin said. "But, fine, we'll pour one out for him instead."

She tilted the flask over the steps where Harrison had died. "To Harrison," Larkin said, one more time. For herself, for him, and for what she had promised to Ed.

The liquid that poured out of Harrison's flask was a very bright blue.

CHAPTER 21

Larkin's first instinct was to wipe up the liquid with the packet of tissues in Harrison's bag—the entire packet, plastic and tissue against the concrete, doing little more than rubbing the liquid directly into the steps. Anni's first instinct was to take the flask from Larkin and screw the lid on tight.

"Blue," Larkin said.

"I know," Anni said.

"Nate-the-nurse said that Rohypnol turned drinks blue."

"Right," Anni said. "Unless Harrison was drinking something that was already blue."

"Like what?" Larkin asked. "A blue margarita? Blueberry wine? A melted slushie from the gas station? No. Obviously not. Somebody put roofies in Harrison's flask."

"Well, we can give the flask to the police and let them figure out who," Anni said.

"Too many fingerprints," Larkin said. "Ours, Harrison's, the nurse's, maybe his grandmother's."

"And maybe his murderer's," Anni said. "The police could figure that out."

"Yes," Larkin said, "but—"

She knew that there was a trustworthy law enforcement representative sitting next to her mother in the first row mezzanine, and she knew that the most sensible thing that she and Anni could do right now would be to put the flask back into Harrison's bag and pass it to Claire Novak after the concert. Except—what if the person who roofied Harrison saw the bag and stole the flask before they could get a chance? Or what if that person saw them carrying the bag and decided to put Rohypnol in her and Anni's water bottles? Maybe now, maybe a month from now—it was too risky. They had to figure out what to do *now* before they figured out what to do *next*.

"Rohypnol is a controlled substance," Larkin said. "Right?"

"Yes," Anni said. "It's illegal in the United States."

"But not everywhere."

"No," Anni said. "Many European countries legally allow Rohypnol, but in most cases you need a doctor's prescription first."

"That chamber choir went to Europe a few summers ago," Larkin said. "Jessalyn was there. Ben. Harrison. They took photos in front of the Eiffel Tower. Could someone have gotten a Rohypnol prescription while they were in Europe?"

"Probably not on one of those seven-countries-in-seven-days things," Anni said. "Plus, they would have had to smuggle it back into the United States."

"That would have been easy," Larkin said. "Customs asks if you have anything to declare, and everyone says no."

"I always tell them," Anni said. "Even if all I did was

buy a pair of socks that one of the nerd bands was selling —and I don't usually buy merch, it's overpriced, but these socks had *toes*—while the nerd cruise was docked in Baja California."

"Why would you have to go through customs in California?"

"Baja California is in Mexico," Anni said. "The band played a live show there, during one of the ports of call."

"Wait," Larkin said. "I remember this. I read it online." Her phone was in her backpack, which required removing Harrison's satchel, which she almost put down on the wet spot before handing it to Anni. "You don't need a prescription to buy roofies in Mexico."

"Why not?"

"Because they sell Rohypnol as a sleeping pill," Larkin said, reconfirming the information on her phone and then sliding it back into her backpack. "Or a relaxation aid. It suppresses adrenaline."

"Which is why the epinephrine injector didn't work," Anni said. "Because Harrison was roofied before he injected himself."

"Is epinephrine the same thing as adrenaline?"

"Yes," Anni said. "It's the pharmaceutical name. Adrenaline is what the body produces naturally, epinephrine is adrenaline you buy in a tube."

"How do you know all of this?"

"I told you, I'm doing an article on adults with peanut allergies—wait!" Anni smiled, in a way that Larkin wouldn't expect someone to smile when confronted with the fact that someone they knew had been drugged in a way that probably led to their death, and the person responsible for the drugging was probably in the building they were currently outside of. "I was going to tell you earlier. Nobody else got sick, the day Harrison died."

"What do you mean?"

"If Marlene really put a batch of peanut-poisoned scotcheroos on the allergen-free table, then other people would have had allergic reactions too. But nobody else got sick. Just Harrison."

"And he really did go into anaphylactic shock," Larkin said. "The police confirmed it."

"Well," Anni said, "I suppose if it were me and I was putting stuff in Harrison's flask to begin with, maybe I'd put some peanut oil in there too."

"So it really was murder," Larkin said.

"It probably really was."

Then Larkin smiled. "And I know who did it."

CHAPTER 22

The Adagio for Strings had already started when they went inside; Barber's agitas rising and falling as they passed the backstage monitors. The choir was lined up, a silent string of men in ties and tails leading towards the women, clustered and whispering, in mismatched black dresses. Someone said "Shhhh!" The strings ascended. Larkin and Anni turned away from the choir and towards the green room.

It was fortunate that Larkin had developed a reputation for being both late and unprepared. "Oh my goodness, I'm so sorry," she said, as the four soloists looked up. "My car ran out of gas, I mean, I ran out of money for gas, I mean, wow, I've got to get changed." She was carrying both her backpack and Harrison's satchel; she swung the latter around, to make sure everyone in the room saw it. "Here, I'll just do it in the bathroom," she said, and handed Harrison's bag to Anni. "Will you hold this for me?"

"Sure," Anni said, executing her one scripted line perfectly. She took the satchel and stood by the door. Two of the soloists did nothing; they had no reason to be concerned by any of this. Jessalyn recognized the bag, but Larkin knew she would make the choice to remain calm; Jessalyn had Adam and the rest of her life ahead of her, after all.

The remaining soloist, just as Larkin predicted, followed her into the bathroom.

The green room bathroom had two stalls and one sink; it was unisex, which meant that Gerald could enter without anyone else thinking it strange. Larkin had already stripped down to her black underwire bra; it would help if she looked a little vulnerable, and it might keep definitely-not-gay Gerald from thinking straight. The Barber played, softly and with much of the bass removed, through a small speaker in the ceiling. They had maybe five minutes.

"Where did you get that bag?" Gerald asked.

"Harrison's grandmother's nurse gave it to me," Larkin said. "Harrison had left a note inside for me, which is why she thought I should have it. His grandmother didn't want anything to do with it. I think she didn't have a very high opinion of her own grandson."

"Who did?" Gerald said, washing his hands at the sink. Larkin thought of Lady Macbeth and knew she had guessed correctly. The only questions remaining were whether Anni could take care of everything else that needed to be completed, on the other side of the bathroom door—which Larkin was fairly certain Anni could, Anni being more competent than anyone else Larkin knew— and whether Larkin could take Gerald in a fight, if it came to it. The only combat Larkin had studied was the stage kind, which meant she knew how to surreptitiously slap her upstage thigh every time she was supposed to slap somebody's face.

"I don't know," Larkin said. "The note Harrison left me was pretty interesting. But you probably already have an idea of what it says."

Gerald was now thinking about all the incriminating things Harrison could have written. Larkin could tell because he washed his hands again, and then wiped them on the sides of his tuxedo pants. "Harrison knew, didn't he," Larkin said. She had to keep Gerald from asking to see the note, which would instantly prove that she had no credibility beyond her own instincts, and she had to get Gerald to say it himself. Anni had explained why, when the two of them were putting their plan into place.

"Knew what?" A good move, on Gerald's part. Anything Larkin said next he could deny, if he wanted to —so she chose the one part of the story that was undeniable.

"You got the job," Larkin said. "The tenure-track music faculty position that both you and Jessalyn were inter- viewing for."

The next step was to cross in front of Gerald and the sink, stand in front of the bathroom door, and lock it. The latter had to be accomplished without Gerald noticing, which meant saying something that would distract him— and Larkin chose "And Jessalyn couldn't interview because she got sick, right?"

Gerald could have said anything—literally *anything*— in response. He chose "It's not my fault Harrison roofied her."

This is where Larkin, if she were operating like the kind of amateur detective who appeared in the mystery section of the Cedar Rapids Public Library, would have replied with "I never said Jessalyn was roofied." But then she remembered Jessalyn hadn't been. "That was what I always thought was odd, when I heard the rumors,"

Larkin continued. "Rohypnol is illegal in the United States."

"So he got it illegally," Gerald said.

"And it turns drinks blue. Jessalyn would have noticed."

"Okay," Gerald said, "so I used roofie in the non-trade-marked sense. Like Kleenex or Xerox or Google."

"I don't think they'd want their brands to be associated with *that*," Larkin said. Then she thought very carefully about how to phrase the next question. "So what got put in Jessalyn's drink instead?"

"Those pills she was always taking," Gerald said. "For her nerves."

"And how would Harrison have done it?"

"He would have taken the pills out of Jessalyn's purse when she wasn't looking, crushed them up, and put them in her drink."

"How would he have gotten into Jessalyn's purse?"

"Jessalyn never watched her purse," Gerald said. "She'd put it on the back of a chair and leave it there."

"And how would Harrison have crushed the pills?"

"Put the pills on a coaster, put your gin and tonic on top of the coaster, and grind the pills under the weight of the glass. Dump the powder from the coaster into the drink. Problem solved."

"Someone would have noticed the pill debris on the coaster."

"They were those cheap disposable bar coasters," Gerald said. "You just throw it away afterwards."

"So that's how Harrison could have done it," Larkin said, "but I don't understand why."

Larkin knew several reasons why Harrison could have done it—she and Anni had come up with them together, after all—but she wasn't asking this question to gain new motives for a person she had always suspected was not a suspect. She was asking this question, just like she had asked all of her other questions, to hear Gerald's answer.

"You already know why," Gerald said. "Because Rohypnol would have turned the drink blue."

When Larkin had thought about somebody drugging Jessalyn, she had always assumed—naïvely, she now understood—that it was the first time they had done anything like that. If this person had both drugged Jessalyn and murdered Harrison, those must also have been first-time offenses (technically, twice for the drugging and first for the murdering). Now she realized that Gerald, who had stopped washing his hands and had crossed them, defensively, over his chest, could be more dangerous than she had previously assumed. Which, to be fair, she should have considered before she locked herself into a bathroom with him.

"I bet he didn't even think of that, when he smuggled the pills over the border," Larkin said. "All that trouble, the worry that you might get caught, drug crimes, jail time, the whole deal, and you can't even use them."

"You can use them," Gerald said. "Just not when someone decides to order a made-up vodka drink with a pickle spear in it."

"Of course," Larkin said, giving Gerald his *yes*. Now she needed the *and*. "So you use Jessalyn's benzodiazepines instead."

"You use fucking whatever," Gerald said. "I would have used aspirin if that was all she had in there."

"That could have killed her," Larkin said.

"She would have gone to the hospital and they would have pumped her stomach."

"Which is what you expected to happen with Harrison."

Larkin watched Gerald register that she knew. She watched his face as it moved from regret to shame to fear; she watched his hands as they pushed their way away from his chest in a gesture of appeal, clasped and twisted as he brought them back close to himself, for protection, and then—leading the expression that soon settled over his entire body—landed on his hips. Shoulders up, elbows out. He had chosen defiance.

"It was an accident," he said.

"You just wanted him to get sick," Larkin said. "Like when they did the Mass in B."

Gerald's left hand left his hip; foundered in the air as if it were looking for an explanation. "You mean the Mass in G," Gerald finally said. "I had nothing to do with that."

I knew it was the Mass in G, Mom, Larkin thought. *I paid attention. I just wanted to throw him off balance.* She wanted to say it aloud, get it on the recording she was currently making on her phone, but she knew that if everything went well, she could tell her mother all about it later. If everything went well, her mother would already know where she was and what she was doing, and would be waiting on the other side of the door when Larkin finally turned around and unlocked it.

But first she had to finish what Gerald had started.

"Why did you want Harrison to get sick?"

"Because he was going to ruin everything," Gerald said. He was wavering, almost entirely split, between the defiant hand on his right side and the lost hand on his left. It clutched at itself, fingers digging into the palm; pressed against Gerald's heart, caught itself in his hair. "The performance, my job, my life."

"Your job," Larkin said, giving his words back to him. "Your life."

"Do you know how much I needed that job?" Gerald

asked, his hand traveling down from his hair to cover his face. "Something else would have worked out for Jessalyn. Things always work out for people like Jessalyn."

"That's the truth," Larkin said. Above them, Barber's strings reached their apex; there was silence, and then the adagio continued. They had two minutes. "So Harrison figured it out, then."

"He cornered me," Gerald said. "At the soloist rehearsal. Said that everyone was on him for putting something in Jessalyn's drink and he was pretty sure he hadn't done it. Then he said he knew exactly one person who had benefited from the tragedy of that evening—he always spoke like that, like he didn't grow up in on a hog farm in the middle of nowhere—and he wanted to ask me if I had anything to say to Jessalyn."

"What did you say?"

"I told him that I had no idea what he was talking about."

"That's fairly cliché," Larkin said. She couldn't help it. She'd almost expected more from Gerald, at this point.

"That's what he said," Gerald continued. "So I told him that he had spent the last god-knows-how-long putting his creepy little piano paws over any bit of fresh meat that walked in the door, it's like he didn't even give the rest of us a chance, and if it ended up coming back to bite him in the ass then I couldn't do anything about it."

"And he said you could." Larkin knew enough about Harrison to presume this. Plus, the Barber was almost over. She couldn't remember how many anguished adagio wobbles the audience had to sit through before they could stand up and applaud, and she hadn't really been counting, but they were very close.

"And I said I wouldn't." Now Gerald's hands were folded across his chest—defensive, but triumphant. "And I told him that if he kept asking questions like that he might not get to play many more rehearsals."

Everything in Larkin's investigation—and Harrison's life—depended on Gerald answering the next question honestly. "And then what did you do?"

"Exactly what I did to Jessalyn," Gerald said. He was smiling, his lips pressed thinly against his teeth in the grin of the aggressor. "I got him out of my way."

Then he took a step forward. "Now," he said, "what am I going to do to you?"

"Absolutely nothing," Larkin said, unlocking the door behind her and giving it a push—thank god it was a push door, she'd had a fifty-percent chance, she'd never forget to check the direction of a door before locking it behind her, ever again—to reveal Officer Novak, her mother, Anni, and Ed.

Over the PA system—and Larkin couldn't have timed it any better if she'd tried—the audience began to applaud.

Gerald glared at Larkin, then walked past her into the green room. Claire Novak stepped into his path and flashed her badge.

"Claire Novak," she said. "We have reason to believe that you have information that can help us with an investigation we're doing into the death of Harrison Tucker. Would you mind coming down to the station with us for a little while?"

"Claire, I'm sending you the recording I made while we were in there." Larkin tapped at her phone, wondering if there were any rules about transmitting evidence to law enforcement over social media direct message. "It was a great conversation."

"You recorded that?" Gerald asked—and Anni jumped in with the answer. "Iowa is a one-party consent state," she said. "That makes it one of 38 states, not including the

District of Columbia, where it's legal to record a conversation without informing people beforehand."

Claire did not put handcuffs on Gerald; instead, she put one firm hand on his shoulder. That was enough. "Want to go have a chat?"

Gerald let Claire walk him halfway to the green room door before he remembered. "I have a performance," he said. "I have to sing."

"That's all been taken care of," Claire said. She kept her eyes on Gerald and let her voice travel to the back of the room. "Thanks for the tip, girls. Jo, I'll be in touch after this gets taken care of. Listen to the Beethoven twice as hard for me."

The applause was over; Claire and Gerald were gone; the green room door stood open, and they could hear the rustles and footsteps of 150 choristers beginning their procession onto the stage. "But—" Ed said, looking around him as if he was still trying to figure out what had happened, "we can't still do the Beethoven."

"Of course we can," Larkin said, waiting for him to figure it out.

"But Gerald's been arrested."

"Technically, he hasn't," Anni said. "But he doesn't know that yet."

"But Gerald killed Harrison."

"Technically, we haven't proven that yet," Anni continued. "While it was legal for Larkin to record Gerald according to the one-party consent rules in the state of Iowa, that kind of amateur phone recording might be considered inadmissible evidence."

"Claire will have to get the confession out of Gerald on her own," Josephine said. Then she blushed. "I'm pretty sure she can do it."

"But we don't have a tenor soloist."

"Yes," Larkin said, "we do."

Then she stepped forward, put both hands on Ed's shoulders, and kissed him.

"Sorry," she said, looking first to Ed and then to her mom. "That was probably inappropriate."

"Out of everything that has happened in the past ten minutes," Ed said, "*that's* what you consider inappropriate?" Then he leaned into Larkin's arms, letting his forehead rest against hers. For a moment, this was all there was—and all that mattered.

"You know the part, I trust?" The interruption came from Josephine, and her voice made it clear that she was speaking not as Larkin's mother, but as Ed's boss.

"Yes, no, well, I mean—" Larkin watched Ed decide that he did, in fact know it. "Yes. I do."

"Well, you have forty-five minutes to get ready," Anni said. "The other soloists are right outside, I already filled them in on the change in plans, they're going to help. Larkin, you and I need to get onstage *right now.*"

"I haven't even put my dress on yet," Larkin said. She had forgotten until that moment that she was only wearing jeans and a bra. At least it was a good bra, one that she wouldn't be embarrassed for her mother or a police officer or a potential murderer or her best friend or the man she had just kissed to see her wearing. It had lace, and no white threads poking out of the seams—unlike the stretched-out, deodorant-stained, Crunchberry-cocktail-splashed-on little black dress she was pulling out of her backpack.

"Put it on over your jeans, they're dark enough," Anni instructed. "And then run."

Anni had the head start, but Larkin's legs were longer; by the time her black sneakers caught up with Anni's black flats, they were just in time to take their places at the tail end of the choir. Out of breath, yes; smiling much too widely for Beethoven, yes; Larkin realizing too late that she had left her folder in the green room and knowing that Anni would share hers.

Now all they had to do was sit through the first three movements of the Ninth Symphony.

CHAPTER 23

Larkin had never really heard Beethoven's Ninth Symphony before. She had listened to it—more often, even, since the day she helped Ed sort music and then wore his shirt home—but it had often been in the context of "while taking the dishes out of the dishwasher and putting them in what would inevitably be the wrong cupboards" or "while staring at a blinking cursor and telling herself she was writing her dissertation."

She had never sat still, with nothing to think about but the music, and *heard* it.

By all good sense she should be thinking of Gerald. She had spent the entirety of the last performance thinking about Marlene. But Marlene had been wrong and Gerald had been right, and so Larkin's brain was no longer interested in what she wasn't doing or what she should be doing or whether everything would work out in the end.

Everything had worked out.

And Larkin's brain was, for the moment, only interested in Beethoven.

The first movement began as an invitation: preparing

the audience, helping them transition into the world the symphony was about to create, strings beckoning the listener to follow them down the path, more and more instruments joining them along the way until, suddenly, they were surrounded by the full orchestra—there it was, an instruction to what was to come, *pay attention, you'll hear this again soon, but by the time you do, you and the music might have changed,* and then the strings were off again, demanding the audience follow along with them.

Larkin had never followed along before. Not with this kind of music. It had always been the background to something more interesting.

There—the full orchestra was back, every talented musician in the Creative Corridor in a major key, welcoming each of the listeners who had followed them so far. The music began to get more complicated, an anxious melody against a steady pulse, before resolving into what Larkin could only view as a reminder: *Love. It's always love. Thank you for paying attention.*

It didn't seem fair that it was *always* love, *always* attention, *always* work; and yet Schiller had not written about the great success of having found a friend, he wrote about the effort it takes to be a friend, the attention required to love someone else, the joy found in this daily work, and the opportunity to share in this joy with everyone else who has made the same discovery.

And Beethoven turned it into a symphony that was rarely performed, due to the work required; and yet it was a piece of music that consistently brought joy to everyone who shared in it.

Especially if they paid attention to the whole thing, not just the parts at the end that they knew.

Because that's what human relationship was, really—a melody that you learned before you ever realized you were learning it, something they taught you in preschool or grade school or your first week of piano lessons, but that was only because as soon as you heard it, you'd say "I know this! It's 'Ode to Joy.'"

And some people stopped there, thinking that was all there was. Larkin had, for longer than it made her comfortable to realize. Anni hadn't—she'd picked up a bit more of it, probably because she'd had a sister and an extended family and a mother who needed them all to help her through chemo and radiation—but Anni had also found a place to stop, a place where she felt comfortable being uncomfortable, not knowing how to make small talk and living alone in her plant-filled room.

Larkin's mother had stopped, too. Turned her face away from people and towards poetry, except in the cases where she could organize individuals like iambs. She'd chosen not to do the work of finding a *hard-won, devoted wife,* as Schiller (or one of his translators) had put it, and part of that may have been due to the fact that the world had only allowed her to have a wife for a short enough period of time that Larkin could still remember the day it happened. Now Larkin's mother was starting again, blushing and letting her hair fall into just enough disarray to prove that she was thinking about someone else besides herself.

And now Larkin had to think about Ed. She didn't know enough about him to know where he was, in all of this; obviously he'd had to figure out how to fit in wherever he went, to be the most sociable man in the room, to be everything to anyone who wanted something from him, and to be none of the things they didn't want. Larkin didn't know what Ed wanted, in a friendship. She wondered if he'd ever asked himself this, or if he'd just assumed he'd have to be friends with everyone, putting in all the effort of *being* while receiving few of the benefits of *friendship*.

She didn't know what Ed wanted out of love, either. Maybe someone who could understand him from the very beginning, a cultural connection deeper than anything Larkin could provide. Maybe someone who could understand him as he was now, an artist trying to help people make art in a community where he was still working to belong. Maybe he and Larkin would end up being everything to each other and maybe they would only end up being very good friends—and either way it would take work, from both of them, and Larkin wasn't sure she knew how to do that kind of work because she was very sure she had never done it before.

Larkin realized she had stopped paying attention to the symphony. Luckily, Beethoven welcomed her back— Larkin almost thought she saw Maestro Kimbrough smile, as she looked up—the orchestra ascending into a new key as the strings and then the winds descended into what Larkin did not want to describe as a *frenzy*, her mother would ask her to find a word that hadn't been used quite so often, but there really was no other word for it, before softening into calmness again.

Tension and release, as Ed had told her—and as she finally understood.

Larkin wondered if this was how everyone was supposed to listen to music, or at least music like this symphony, which was currently adding tension to its gentle melodic line by interspersing what she might call "string fanfares," except she was pretty sure that Ed and Anni and half the people on the stage with her (including all of the strings) had a better word for what was going on. Larkin didn't know any of the classical music words, only the musical theater ones, and she wasn't sure she knew how to listen to music when there wasn't a singer telling her exactly what to feel, *cry, don't cry, follow your dreams,* because every time she tried to pay attention to Beethoven's patterns—there, he was repeating *sol-do* cadences, she could thank her sixth-grade music teacher and *The Sound of Music* for teaching her what a *sol-do* cadence was—she found herself distracted away from the mechanics of the symphony by the simple fact that it was making her feel things.

And think about things.

Mostly, the things she was feeling.

The not-paying-attention Larkin was doing at the moment was different than the not-paying-attention she had done at the last performance and nearly every choral rehearsal. She couldn't have told you, then, whether one of the horns had played a wrong note or whether the music had been fast or slow or whether a dog had run across the stage. She could have told you, now, that whatever Beethoven was doing with his symphony was a lot like what he had done at the beginning of the movement, the excited *come-along-come-along-come-along* pattern that had prompted her to start following along in the first place, but all of that was only making her think of how much she wanted to tell Ed about it later. How she had listened, or tried to listen, and how it had made her think about everything she had just done—no, she didn't want to think about that, catching a murderer was too distracting—and everything Ed must be doing right now, and everything she wanted to ask him about *how to listen to music* as soon as she had the chance, except the music was happening right now, and she was trying so hard to pay attention that she kept missing bits of it.

Unless that was how you were supposed to listen to Beethoven.

Then the music slowed down, and something changed with the rhythm; some of the strings began dragging some of their notes longer than they ought to go, carrying them through as the orchestra kept moving, a circular synchronicity that caught itself together and then came apart again. This held Larkin in place, silent and almost in awe, until the strings reunited in quiet contemplation and invited her to do the same.

Ed—who would know everything about what she had just heard—would be backstage, maybe taking himself through the same warmups he had led at the beginning of every choral rehearsal, maybe going through his score and making notes on where to breathe, maybe singing the entire solo through just to make sure he could do it, maybe skipping all of the tension parts and going straight to the part where he walks out onto the stage, relaxed, knowing he has everything he needs to get through the fourth movement on his own, with Jessalyn and Shawnta and Ben by his side and Larkin at his back and his parents out in the audience. They would be surprised. Maestro Kimbrough would be surprised. Everyone in the entire orchestra hall, except Larkin and Anni and Larkin's mother, would be surprised—and Larkin, unsurprisingly, had lost track of the music again.

So she renewed her focus, resolving to pay attention to every detail. She heard Beethoven alter his melody so that the tension stretched beyond the initial four-note repetition; a circular pattern becoming linear and then extending and then ascending and then descending and then unifying into a single tone.

And then, as it was at the beginning, *come along, come along, come along.* Or, now that Larkin knew the figure well enough to be familiar with it, *here we are, here we are, here we are.*

Here, the orchestra restated, loudly and with emphasis. *This is real. This is what is happening now, in this room. This piece, that people have worked together to learn and perform for two hundred years. Listen, because this is worth paying attention to.*

By the end of the first movement, Larkin was exhausted. She welcomed the break, the breath, the part of the symphony she had never noticed before because it was never part of the recording. The silence, the cough, the soft shift as the maestro brought the orchestra to attention again.

Larkin sat up straight, just like the musicians. She was ready.

The second movement had always been Larkin's favorite. A trio of shattering octaves interrupted by drums, followed by the kind of melody that felt as alive as thought, as real as heartbeat. A dance. An idea. A truth, somehow; every flower that had ever pulled itself out of the ground and every person who had ever pushed themselves into doing something difficult.

The tune was as familiar as "Ode to Joy," Larkin was sure she had heard it in a hundred movies somewhere, but nobody had put words to it.

Yet.

You caught a, you caught a, murderer, murderer, you and your friends caught a murderer, murderer, Larkin sang to herself, wishing she could whisper it to Anni—except Anni, at that moment, was also immersed in her own musical interpretation, shoulders and thigh muscles and fingertips twitching to match the timpani, her whole body joining the dance while sitting perfectly still. They were both smiling; all of the audience members who were sitting close enough to be captured by the footlights were smiling; Larkin dared to look quickly behind her and saw that everyone in the megachoir who was currently paying attention to the music was smiling. The rest were staring, slack-faced, at nothing. Waiting without listening. Missing it all.

You caught a, you caught a, murderer, murderer
You and your friends caught a murderer, murderer
YOU DID, said the strings.
WE DID, echoed the drums.
HE DID IT, HE DID IT, HE DID IT, the horns called, louder and louder.

It was over too soon; Maestro Kimbrough dropped his arms and wiped his brow, and everyone in the room who had been paying attention exhaled. Anni reached out to stop Larkin's hands before she could start to applaud.

The third movement—Larkin had never understood it, and she started off trying to understand it, but her mind instantly fell into the places it always did when Beethoven's adagio pulled its way into her playlist, which was why she usually skipped the track and moved on to the fourth-movement finale. That, and the third movement was twenty minutes long. The same as an episode of whatever Larkin would rather be watching, because anything she could think of was literally better than listening to this slow, *molto slow*, achingly immemorable piece of music.

She couldn't tell you its melody if she tried.

But that was probably because the third movement, every single time, made her think about everything she was trying very hard not to remember.

This time she gave herself over to it, because maybe that was the point of the thing, maybe she'd learn something by letting her mind go wherever Beethoven wanted it to, which just happened to be all of the places she didn't want it to go, because most of them started with her dissertation and the acknowledgment that she would never, ever finish it.

Not because she couldn't, though maybe that was part of it.

Because she didn't want to.

Because she'd picked the wrong path, from the beginning—from the day some beleaguered theater faculty member had looked at Larkin, calculated her hypotenuse and her complete lack of threats, and asked her if she'd ever considered directing, and Larkin had picked that path because she hadn't been brave enough to say *no, I want to be on stage.*

And then, later, she picked the academic path because she hadn't been brave enough to say *no, I want to try and make it in the professional theater world, and if I don't make it, I'll find something else to do.*

And all of those wrong paths had led to dead ends.

The one time she had felt like she was on the right path, out of all the years she'd spent pushing herself forward, was the summer she spent studying with Anne Bogart. Her faculty adviser had advised against it; this was a camp for actors, and Larkin was not an actor. But Larkin said *no, the website says it's for anyone who is interested in understanding how theater works, they specifically say they don't care about body type or background or resumes, they just want people who are ready to focus and practice and learn.*

Those three weeks were the hardest Larkin had ever focused. They studied the physical mechanics of the body, doing exercises that activated one muscle group after another, completing impossible tasks like sitting in an invisible chair. They were not allowed to stand again until they had made all the necessary right angles, and at the time Larkin thought how wonderful it was that someone had given them something concrete and difficult and specific to do and not let them stop until they'd done it.

And then the next day her legs hurt, all over, but they spent the morning stretching and it worked itself out.

They also studied the mechanics of human interaction, which was even more central to theater than storytelling. The story barely mattered, they were told; you could perform something as predictable and ridiculous as *A Midsummer Night's Dream* as long as each individual moment was honest and specific and grounded in true, recognizable human behavior. As long as the audience could see themselves and understand themselves and use that understanding to become better selves, the story could be anything.

They built plays out of nonsense words; they created scenes that used no words at all; they improvised until somebody did something cliché or contrived or lazy or dishonest and then they were told to stop.

Because they were there to make art—and art, like beauty, could only come from truth.

Now Larkin understood the truth of her current situation: that she would never be an academic, that she might never be a director, that she would never get to have "doctor" appended in front of her name. She would have to do something else instead, and that was wonderful because she would get to do something else instead, and this time it would be based on something real, not something she was only doing because it was a substitute for what she really wanted.

She still wanted to make art, in the sense that she wanted to make something real and beautiful that helped people understand the truth about the world, but since it felt like she had only started understanding the truth about the world in the past two months, maybe that would have to wait for a bit. In the meanwhile she would have to earn money—and she knew exactly where she would go, the very next morning if she could, to ask for a job. The sign had only been in the coffee shop window for a day; Larkin had noticed it as she rode her mother's bike to the orchestra hall. If she got there as soon as they opened, maybe the position wouldn't yet have been filled.

Larkin wondered if her mother would be embarrassed that her daughter, who had previously had such a promising career trajectory, was now interested in working at a local coffee shop. But Larkin had years of experience in food service, she knew how to work an espresso machine, and this wasn't going to be her only job. The sign in the window had said they were looking for part-time workers. The rest of the time—well, she'd have to talk to Anni about that, and Ed, and maybe even her mother if she felt brave enough.

At that moment, as Beethoven's horns ascended like water rising from a fountain, like a person suddenly understanding the truth, the release of being allowed to stand up and walk away from the terrible invisible chair, Larkin felt brave enough to do anything.

Which meant it was time for the fourth—and final— movement. The orchestra paused; Maestro Kimbrough gave a quick glance stage left. Jessalyn led the way, resplendent in shimmering blue; Shawnta followed, in patterned pink and gold; then Ben, not wearing the tuxedo he had worn in the previous performance, but the simple, understatedly expensive trousers and jacket he had brought to change into, afterwards. A white shirt, with collar; no tie.

Then Ed. The flash of excitement on his face was instantly absorbed by the audience and—more impor- tantly—the choir that he had spent so many weeks instructing. Larkin did not need to turn around, this time, to see who was paying attention. She could feel their energy, as Ed looked first towards them, then towards her, then to Maestro Kimbrough. A single eyebrow was raised, followed by a hand. The choir stood. The orchestra put bows, fingers, and valves in their appropriate places. Maestro Kimbrough raised his other hand, inviting them all to make music together.

It began.

The fourth movement started in dissonance; the only way it could begin, after the somnambulant harmony of the third. Violins in anguish, basses in uncertainty, trumpets calling out for an answer to the question, the only question, *how does one live, what should one do, I am joyless in this indifferent world and I do not know how to change.* The violins replied, more softly—*listen.* The basses—*hear.* The full orchestra, echoing the theme of the second movement —*the world is not indifferent, the world is not joyless, the world is life and discovery and growth.* Then the third movement —*be brave, because you know what must be done.*

And then, at last, the melody.

The one part of the Ninth Symphony that everybody in the entire room knew.

It soared through the orchestra first, reminding everyone of its existence, reminding them that this was why they had gathered together in this room. A triumphant collection of experiences coalescing in this shared experience, this celebration of the work required to make joy.

Then the dissonance again, because Beethoven wanted to draw the listeners together in tension before the ultimate release. Ben, stepping forward, looking straight out into the darkness—*O Freunde, nicht diese Töne!* Anyone who was paying attention knew exactly what he was singing even if they didn't know the German, because it came through in his voice and his posture and the way his feet connected with the ground. *Friends, Ben sang, enough of this anxiety and uncertainty. Pay attention, because we are going to share the secret of a joyful life.*

And they did. Ben, the basses, the tenors, and then the four soloists, Jessalyn and Shawnta and Ed stepping forward to join in unified quartet. They were all carrying their folders, this time; the three soloists who had their music memorized covering for the one who still needed a little extra help. That was part of the joy, though nobody except Larkin and Anni and Larkin's mother knew why—and Schiller, he had written why it was part of the joy two hundred years ago, and now they were sharing in this rediscovered discovery together.

Joy—and music—reuniting what had been driven apart by fear and jealousy and grievance. *Friends until the end,* Larkin sang, sharing Anni's music, secure in her sylla-bles. *The kind of love that takes a lifetime to learn and lasts even beyond death.*

And then it was time for Ed's solo.

If Ben had called the audience to attention, Ed invited them to ascend beyond whatever mental spaces consti-tuted *hearing* and enter the truth of *knowing.* His voice was confident, pure, untroubled by anything that must have been occupying his mind over the past forty-five minutes. This was his message, and Beethoven's, and Schiller's, and now it was yours—*joy comes to those who do the work.* His tenor leapt between intervals as if singing this solo and sharing this music were the only thing he had been put on this earth to do; as if his entire life had brought him to this moment.

Which it had.

And then it was the choir's turn to join him, and Larkin

could hardly get the notes out for smiling. She swiped at an eye, noticing the wetness before she registered the tears, and Anni handed her one of the tissues that were of course tucked into one of the pockets of the choir folder, and Larkin ran the tissue over her eyes and under her nose and kept singing, because every voice counted and she was not going to let hers falter.

It was over—a hundred-fifty voices resolving glorious harmony into perfect unison, the cymbals crashing every beat in front of them—before she wanted it to be. The audience was on its feet before Maestro Kimbrough's hands had fully landed at his sides; his face, when he turned to look at them, was as astonished as Beethoven's must have been, that very first time the symphony was performed. He had expected competence and received excellence; the audience, who had expected nothing more than a generalized, dull evening of arts appreciation bolstered by the feeling that they were doing their part for the community, had received a new understanding of joy.

There were bows, there were flowers, there was Anni's wet tissue against Larkin's nose and then a second tissue pressed into her hand, and then—after even more applause and another set of bows—a finger poked into Larkin's side.

"You need to lead us off the stage," Anni whispered.

Larkin—who had trained to be a director but had never really thought of herself as a leader before—did exactly that.

Because after that night, she could do anything.

CHAPTER 24

After it was all over—after Larkin had met Ed's parents and been introduced to what appeared to be the entirety of Anni's extended family, Libbi and her husband and their twins Dax and Pax ("wow, you got your stitches out!"), followed by Mimi and Pop-Pop and the other grandpa, Plop-Plop ("that was Dax's idea") and Anni's indomitable mother and slightly more domitable father ("I don't know if I'd call myself a classical music person, but there's something about that song that makes you really glad to be alive"), after Larkin had accepted a crushed-chiffon embrace from Jessalyn ("thank you, thank you") and a slight nod from the Maestro and helped everyone put away the chairs and restack the music stands—after there was nothing left to do in the orchestra hall, they went to the police station.

Larkin and Anni on their respective bikes, and Josephine and Ed in their respective cars.

"Well, we got what we needed out of our prime suspect," Claire Novak said, meeting them in the lobby with cardboard-sheathed cups of coffee that only Larkin and her mother accepted. "He's made a full confession."

"What happens now?" Josephine asked, and Larkin watched Claire soften, for just an instant, before snapping back into professionality. "The legal system," she said. "We're holding him for now, but he'll get a lawyer, he'll probably post bail, he'll either plea bargain or go to trial."

"You can plea bargain for murder?" That was from Ed.

"You can plea bargain for anything," Claire said. "Saves the courts a ton of time and saves the taxpayers a ton of money."

"It doesn't save the taxpayers anything," Anni said. "We pay taxes based on income."

"You kids," Claire said, smiling. "Smart as anything."

"I'm nearly forty years old," Anni said.

"You're thirty-seven," Larkin said back.

Claire let that go. "Jo, did you know they figured it all out on their own?"

"I had no idea any of this was going on."

"We're scheduled to get the tox analysis back on Monday," Claire continued. "Autopsies, it's not like you see on TV. Takes some time to get the full report, especially if the deceased isn't very high on the priority list. We assumed it was plain old anaphylactic shock, that's still probably going to be the official cause of death, but we'll be able to confirm whether Rohypnol was involved."

"And peanut oil," Anni said. "Is there a law against knowingly giving someone a substance they're deathly allergic to?"

"I think homicide covers that one," Claire said. "Or manslaughter, depending. Gerald's still arguing that he didn't know Harrison would die. Hoping to get involuntary, I'm guessing. Of course, he'll still have to deal with the drug smuggling and rape charges, assuming we can get some of the other women he roofied to testify."

"The other women?" That was Ed, again.

"I wondered about that," Larkin answered. "I figured it out in the bathroom. It was a mistake to assume that he would have only drugged Jessalyn and Harrison and nobody else. Especially when he was so obsessed with, like, getting women to like him."

"That is not how you get women to like you!" Anni said.

"He actually bragged about that part," Claire said. "Going back to women who had rejected him and convincing them to change their minds, as he put it. He was so proud that none of them had reported. Like it was proof that he had done the right thing."

"Wow," Ed said. "That man was part of our community. I had no idea. I worked with him—I spent weeks coaching him on that solo—I wrote him a letter of recommendation! What am I supposed to do now?"

"Go home," Claire said. "You've done everything you need to do, and we'll take it from here." She turned back to Larkin's mother; this time, she let both her face and her posture soften. "Jo—I'm so sorry to have missed our first date."

"I would call this a reasonable excuse," Josephine said.

"I've got some paperwork to finish up," Claire continued. "Then—I don't know—are you a beer person? A wine person?"

"Mostly, I'm a coffee person," Josephine said. "But I do enjoy a good bourbon."

"If you're still interested, twenty minutes from now," Claire said, "I could pick you up?"

Larkin mentally crossed her fingers, waiting for her mother to say it. "I think you already have."

That made everyone laugh—a necessary, concluding laugh—and then Larkin said "I should go, I have a 7:30 a.m. job interview tomorrow," and her mother said "You have a job interview?" and Larkin said "It's not exactly an interview, it's a Help Wanted sign in the coffee shop below Anni's apartment, I'll tell you if I get it," and then she turned to Anni and said "Will you ride home with me? Since we're both taking the bike trail?" and then Ed said "I could probably put both of your bikes on the back of my car, it's got a bike rack," and then Larkin's mother said "Larkin can put her bike in the trunk of my car, I'm going back home first, I have to get ready for my date," and she fluffed her hair and tossed one shoulder back and made everybody laugh again.

"Ed," Josephine said, "I'll see you on campus. Your solo was excellent, and I've made a note of it."

"Pun intended," Ed said.

"Larkin," her mother continued, "come with me, and tell me about this coffee shop thing."

"Don't be mad," Larkin said.

"Do I look mad?" Larkin's mother asked, smiling. "You're voluntarily choosing to become gainfully employed. I'm thrilled!" Then she turned to Anni. "It's very good to finally meet you. I wish I had met you earlier, because Larkin has mentioned you pretty much every day since—"

"What about Marlene?" Larkin said, suddenly remembering, knowing she was interrupting. "Claire, I mean, Officer Novak, Marlene's going to be okay, right?"

"Who?" Larkin watched Claire remember. "Oh, the woman who came in on Saturday. We took her statement, told her to go home. We already had the results on the stomach contents, there was no indication that Harrison had eaten any baked goods before he died."

"You don't bake a scotcheroo," Larkin said. "You melt all the stuff, the peanut butter and the corn syrup and whatever, and spread it over the rice cereal."

Everyone looked at her.

"What?" Larkin said. Then she twitched her nose at her mother. "See? I paid attention to the details."

"I suppose I have to say I'm impressed," her mother said, twitching her nose back.

"Can I call Marlene?" Larkin continued, directing her question towards Claire. "Just to see how she's doing? Will that be a problem with the investigation or anything?"

"Shouldn't be," Claire said.

"I guess I don't know her phone number."

"It's in the choir directory," Anni said. "I'll forward it to you."

"Great," Larkin said. "Thank you."

"Wait, how is Marlene involved with all of this?" Ed asked.

"She isn't," Larkin said. "She just thought she was. I'll tell you later, okay?"

"We should go," Larkin's mother said. "I can't go on my date until we get out of this lobby and Claire finishes up her paperwork!"

"Get out of here, y'all," Claire said. Then she smiled, one more time, at Larkin's mother. "Jo, I told you—you've got a great kid, and she's made some great friends."

CHAPTER 25

Larkin could have texted Anni when she arrived at the apartment, but someone was already waiting for the elevator—so when the doors slid open, Larkin slid inside and said "Five?" and watched as the person swiped their keycard and took them both up to the floor where only one of them belonged. Technically, Larkin had been invited, which was like being asked to belong—and Larkin still didn't know how she felt about that, not the part where Anni had invited her up for a visit, she felt very good about that part, but the part where she was maybe just a little bit belonging in Pratincola. She had always wanted to belong somewhere —and even though Larkin had never imagined *somewhere* being *Eastern Iowa*, after finishing up her morning shift at the coffee shop and emailing Ed and having lunch with her mother and going for a bike ride around the lake, she was starting to see the value of living in the Creative Corridor.

She might even create something, soon.

But first, she would sneak into Anni's apartment

building and connive her way up to the fifth floor. For old times' sake.

Anni opened the door before she could knock. "I heard your footsteps," she said, as an explanation. She was wearing a blue hoodie with "MATH" printed across the front, and pajama bottoms patterned with what appeared to be decorative autumnal gourds.

Larkin was wearing her favorite pair of jeans and a soft black sweater her mother had bought for her (she had pretended like she didn't need her mom to buy her any new clothes, but both of them had known it was a lie). It felt like a mix of who she had been and who she might become.

"You are welcome to any of the teas in my cupboard," Anni said, as Larkin sat down on what she now thought of as "her side" of the sofa, "but I also have coffee. Regular and decaf."

"Did you start drinking coffee?"

"No, of course not." Anni switched on her electric kettle and smiled. "It's for you. It's the same kind they serve downstairs. I mean, I bought it from them. I was going to buy it from you—I don't think baristas work on commission, but just in case—but your shift was already over. I also bought some pumpkin spice syrup and milk and whipped cream. From the grocery."

"Wow," Larkin said. "You really went all out."

"Well, that's what you're supposed to do, when you're hosting someone in your home," Anni said. "You're supposed to make them comfortable. And if you already know what they like, then that's even better."

"Thank you." Larkin felt—it was hard to say. Loved. Seen. Happy. "I mean, I would have been happy with just plain coffee."

"Good, then I won't buy the extras again once you've

used those up," Anni said, carefully leveling a tablespoon of coffee grounds into a filter before placing it over what Larkin had already started to think of as "her mug," even though it was emblazoned with an investment company logo and Larkin still had to pay off her credit card debt before she could even think about investing. She had just made her first more-than-minimum payment in a year.

"The pumpkin spice syrup contains no actual pumpkin and the whipped cream contains no actual cream," Anni continued, taking the former out of the cupboard and setting it next to the mug. "It's all just corn syrup and chemicals."

"Hey, those are my favorite flavors!" Larkin stood up to help Anni with the coffee, since it looked dangerously close to being well-balanced. She dumped another pile of grounds into the filter before opening the freezer for the whipped cream. "The one good thing about living in Iowa is getting my corn syrup, like, locally grown."

"The one good thing?" Anni poured hot water into her mug, then handed the kettle to Larkin. "Don't tell Dr. Ed you said that."

"I still don't know what I'm going to do about Ed," Larkin said. "I like him, but what if I, like, *double like* him? I don't know how to be that way with people."

"I didn't know how to be a friend," Anni said, "so I looked it up online, and then I went down to the coffee shop to buy pre-ground regular and decaf coffee and then I rode my bike to Hy-Vee to get the syrup and the whipped cream and the filter."

"But we would have been friends without that." Larkin lifted the filter off her coffee mug, added a five-second dash of pumpkin spice syrup and scooped out just enough whipped cream to stick to her nose when she took her first sip. "I mean, this is great, I cannot tell you how much I appreciate this cup of coffee right now, but we were friends when you were suggesting I drink poop tea."

"Well, then, if you and Ed are meant to like-like each other, it'll just happen."

"But what if I don't want it to happen?" Larkin wiped her nose and licked the whipped cream off her knuckle. "Because"—she sat down—"because liking Ed would mean I'd have to stay here, right? And I'm still not sure I want to do that."

"What do you want to do instead?"

"I don't know," Larkin said. She took another sip of her coffee and another swipe of her nose. "That's a lie. I do know, but I don't know how to make it happen."

Anni wrapped her hands around her mug, which was actually an oversized purple teacup covered in geometric blue swirls. "What is it? If you don't mind my asking."

"No, of course not," Larkin said. "I was kind of hoping you could help. Since you know about running a business and all."

"That is true," Anni said. "What kind of business do you want to run?"

Larkin looked down at her mug, then back up at Anni. "I was thinking I might like to become a private detective. I looked it up online, and there aren't any formal requirements for becoming a private investigator in Iowa, except applying for the license and getting your business set up. Other states require you to have a criminal justice degree or a previous career in law enforcement, and maybe I should look into the degree part anyway, or talk to Claire about it. I still haven't told anyone—except you, I guess— because it might be a terrible idea, and it would definitely require me to stay in Iowa, and what am I going to do in Iowa?"

"Help people," Anni said. "And I'll help you get started."

———

Ed rang the doorbell a little before eight; Larkin had hoped to beat her mother to the door, but she was still in her mess of a guest bedroom, with one last piece of her long dark hair wrapped around the curling iron.

So she heard the bell ring again, and then she heard her mother say "I'll get it!" and then she heard her mother laugh. Larkin pulled the curling iron out of her hair and quickly yanked back a fistful of ringlets, holding them back by—what else—the barrette that was still on her nightstand. She looked at herself in the mirror. Her bedazzled "theater kid" tank top peeked from underneath an old white bathrobe. Ed, she knew from his email, would be wearing a tuxedo T-shirt and a Phantom mask. It would be a look, for both of them, and she could only imagine what her mother was looking at.

And there they were, Larkin's mother offering Ed a glass of water or tea or juice or milk or soda—"anything but alcohol, unless Larkin's driving"—and Ed accepting his tumbler of water mostly to be polite, his eyes turning away from the sink as soon as Larkin entered the room. She saw one side of his face blush.

"Hey, Larkin," he said.

"Hey," Larkin said, her voice suddenly having trouble getting from the beginning to the end of the syllable. She hadn't been sure, until that moment, whether Ed had actually asked her on a date or not. He'd originally offered to drive her to the Halloween party so Larkin wouldn't have to waste any more of her available credit on gas. Then, over a series of back-and-forth emails, they'd decided to wear matching costumes.

"Well, don't you both look. . . *lovely*," Josephine said, sizing up the situation instantly, even though Larkin had explained to her that it was okay, Christine and the Phantom weren't endgame, they were just two weird friends who liked music and theater a whole lot. Then she'd had to explain to her mother what endgame was.

"When the symphony invites you to a Halloween-themed fundraising gala," Ed said, trying to maintain his professional composure in front of Dean Day, "you go all out."

"Or you match your going-out look to what the person you're going with can afford," Larkin said. She had told Ed she couldn't buy anything new for this gala, they couldn't do formal or semi-formal or anything that wasn't already in one of Larkin's very-nearly-unpacked boxes, and he had assured her that their novelty T-shirts would fit right in.

"I suppose this is where I say *have her back by midnight*," Larkin's mother said, "but honestly I don't care. You two are adults. Go have fun."

———

Larkin didn't know what to expect, walking into the orchestra hall with Ed at her side and then, after he offered, on his arm. Much of it was exactly as she could have predicted—the familiar folding tables covered with white linens and catering, the easels that held posters announcing the upcoming season and the various benefits associated with each donation tier, the opportunity to enter a costume contest and win two tickets to an upcoming performance. The basket, with the stack of printer paper that someone had sliced into strips, inviting people to vote for their favorite costumes.

The arm—and the way Ed held it out while holding her gaze with both his masked and open eye—was the first surprise.

The second surprise was how many people went out of their way to say hello to her.

At first Larkin assumed they were saying hello to Ed. He was the draw, after all—the choral conductor who had saved the Ninth Symphony with his extraordinary voice, a rapidly-rising Corridor star.

But people kept coming over to talk to Larkin, even after Ed excused himself to do some kind of press thing with Maestro Kimbrough—who Larkin had assumed would arrive dressed as Herr Beethoven, but was in fact wearing a Raygun shirt that read "this is my Halloween costume." The two of them stood side-by-side for photographs, and then Larkin stopped paying attention to whatever Ed and the Maestro were doing because she was too busy paying attention to everyone else.

First, Ben and his silver fox, dressed as Dorothy and the Scarecrow. "Mitchell, come meet the new girl," Ben said. "You look fabulous," he said to Larkin. "I saw you and Ed come in. We should do Phantom and Christine next year, what do you think?"

Mitchell, whose Scarecrow costume was nearly identical to the one worn by Ray Bolger, evaluated Larkin's outfit with the same critical eye she assumed he applied to watches and yachts. "No. Her look is too memorable. Give it at least two years."

"Fine, you're no fun," Ben said. Then, to Larkin, "Actually, he's very fun. You should come by the house sometime. I heard you worked with Anne Bogart, which means you have to hear my opera."

"Opera *in progress*," Mitchell said.

"The best creative works are never finished," Ben said. "Schubert. Mozart's Requiem. *Candide*."

"*Edwin Drood*," Larkin said, even though she'd only seen the musical version.

"See?" Ben said. "She's one of us."

"He's right about these things," Mitchell said.

"We're going to have you over, there will be wine, there will be music, Mitchell has a very serviceable tenor, and then you can tell me what you think," Ben continued. Larkin agreed—they actually set a tentative date—and then Mitchell said "See you soon, then. By the way, I'm voting for your costume."

"Oh, you shouldn't," Larkin said. "I'm with Ed. We're not entering."

"I told you!" Ben said to Mitchell. "Shawnta owes me a drink." Then, to Larkin, "Bring Ed along, if he wants to come. Tell him we'll get that Malbec he likes."

After Ben and Mitchell left—almost immediately after —Larkin saw Jessalyn and Adam. They were reprising their American Gothic look, complete with pitchfork. "This woman saved my life," Jessalyn told Adam. "Larkin, I cannot tell you how well I've been sleeping lately. It's, like, you freed me from all kinds of bad memories that I never knew whether or not were even real."

It was true—Jessalyn looked more rested, more relaxed, more comfortable in her own skin than Larkin had ever seen her. It was funny how she'd thought, when she first met Jessalyn, that Jessalyn had everything. That was just something Jessalyn had put over herself, like makeup, to share on social media. Now she really did appear to have everything she wanted.

Nearly everything, anyway. "I was wondering if you wanted to get coffee sometime," Jessalyn said. "They're asking if I want to interview for that job—you know, the one Gerald had."

"The one Gerald stole from you," Adam said.

"We don't know that," Jessalyn said. "All he did was make sure I didn't get a chance. Now they're giving me one, and I'm not sure I want to take it. I like the life I have now. I'm happy."

"You are happy," Larkin said, because Jessalyn so obviously was.

"But what if I'm turning down the possibility for something even better?" Jessalyn asked. "We should talk, because you're the only other person I know who stepped away from that world."

"I'm not sure I'd be the best person to give advice," Larkin said. "I kinda work at that coffee shop now."

"Don't cut yourself down just because you think someone else will," Jessalyn said. "You're one of the most impressive people I know. I'll text you, okay?"

Next was Marlene, who was wearing a full-body Winnie-the-Pooh costume that had obviously seen multiple Halloweens. She didn't say much—she and Larkin had already had the conversation they needed to have—but she reached into her purse and pulled out a Tupperware packed with scotcheroos.

"No peanut butter," she said.

"Thank you," Larkin said—and then, trusting her instincts, gave Marlene the warmest embrace she had.

Ed was back by the time Carla Ramirez Buckholtz found Larkin. The Buckholtzes had done a family costume; Carla, dressed as Black Widow, had a Captain America clinging to one leg and a pint-sized Incredible Hulk in her arms. "Larkin!" Carla said. "And—I'm so sorry—I can't remember your name."

"Ed Jackson."

"Right," Carla said. "You were one of the pallbearers. Wow—I cannot believe—you know they told me, they keep contacting me about these things, it's like the *ex* in ex-wife doesn't even matter, they said you solved Harrison's murder?"

"I mean," Larkin said, "I didn't. I just helped the police with their investigation."

"You totally did," Ed said. "She was brilliant," he explained to Carla. "Got a full confession out of the guy and recorded it on her phone."

"Which, I mean, it might have been inadmissible," Larkin said, feeling once again a little intimidated by Harrison's ex-wife. Carla's Black Widow costume revealed the kind of fit, toned body Larkin wished she were hiding underneath her battered white robe.

"Wait," Carla said. "The day you met me at that coffee shop—that was part of the investigation, wasn't it?"

"Um. . ." Larkin didn't know what to say. Luckily, Carla saved her from having to make a choice. "I knew it! A girl like you—never would have fallen for Harrison."

Larkin didn't want to admit that she almost had—though she wondered how much of that had been because of the disparity between who she was then and who she was trying to be. Now, for better or worse, she was mostly the same person.

"*Mom,*" Captain America said. "Let's go get *candy.*"

"Mommy's in the middle of a conversation," Carla said.

"Here," Ed said, reaching into his pocket and pulling out a symphony-branded sucker. "Sorry," he said, turning up to Carla, "I should have asked."

"It's okay," Carla said, taking the sucker from Ed and handing it to her son. "I'd say I don't let my child take candy from strangers, but I don't think any of us are strangers anymore."

"BEN! OWES! ME! A! DRINK!"

It was Shawnta, who was wearing what appeared to be a handcrafted tutu made of pleated sheet music. She had an enormous treble clef hanging from one ear and a matching bass clef from the other. "I told him, I told him, hi Captain America, hi baby Bruce, hi Natasha, I said you two would start seeing each other and he said I was seeing things."

"Bye," Carla said, taking her children and waving the few free fingers she could spare.

"BEN!" Shawnta said, turning around to look for him. On the backside of her costume, she had taken the top half of a collapsible metal music stand and bent it into a pair of wings.

"Wow," Ed said. "I'd vote for her outfit, but I'm pretty sure board members and staff can't vote."

"I'll vote for her," Larkin said—and then Ben arrived, with Mitchell, and there was some mutual gushing about who looked fabulous and who had been right all along and who was buying whom a cocktail.

"How about I buy you both a drink?" Ed suggested. "It's probably time to get in line for our plastic cups of boxed wine anyway."

"Sometimes I hate supporting the arts," Ben said. "But let's go and get it over with."

"At this point I've lost track of who lost which bet," Mitchell said. "Shall we say the whole thing is my treat?"

Ben stood on ruby-red tiptoes and kissed him. "I love it when you say that."

Mitchell and Ben led the way, with Shawnta and Ed following—Ed turned and held out his arm again, for Larkin to take or maybe for her to slip her hand against his, she didn't know and she didn't have time to decide because she saw Anni, in the crowd, wearing her skeleton pajamas and staring at her phone and looking happier than Larkin had ever seen her.

And, also, a bit bewildered.

"Anni!" Larkin said.

Anni looked up—looked down at her phone again—looked up and saw Larkin and carefully buttoned her phone into the pocket next to her hipbone.

"Come on," Larkin said, "we're going to get drinks, Ed's here, they're all here—" She turned around. "Well, I guess we're going to have to go find them."

Anni, smiling like she had just read the one phone message that everyone dreams they're going to get to read someday, reached out and hugged Larkin. It was more physical contact than Larkin had ever seen Anni initiate, and it came without any hesitation or flinch.

"Luckily," Larkin continued, "we're detectives! And I. . . um. . . detect that there's something different about you?"

"I got an email," Anni said. "From a very dear friend."

"Right," Larkin said. "A very dear friend whose email is making you look like a giddy schoolgirl."

"It's nothing," Anni said. "Yet. But I'll tell you about it soon. Right now, we need to enjoy this party, because it is important to be part of the community and support the symphony and get to know people who might want to be our clients someday."

"Agreed," Larkin said. "But you have to tell me about it after the party. Or tomorrow."

"Only if you promise one thing," Anni said, the two of them walking towards the drinks line, waving at Ed so he knew they were coming.

"Okay," Larkin said.

"Don't tell anyone I wore my pajamas to a symphony

gala," Anni said. "I've been telling everyone they're just my costume."

"Anni!" Larkin said, putting her hand to her heart in mock surprise—or maybe actual surprise, she wasn't sure. "Are you suggesting we lie?"

"I'm suggesting we create the world we want to live in," Anni said. "And in this world, my pajamas can be a costume and I can get in touch with an old friend and help you solve mysteries and form your first LLC."

"And I can go on a date with Ed and help my friend tell her first lie and help Ben work on his opera and pay off my credit cards and become a private detective and—"

They were at the end of the line, Ed and Ben and Shawnta all motioning them to take a few steps forward.

"And cut in line," Anni said.

"Sorry," Larkin said to the people behind her.

"It's all right," one of them said—a young woman, dressed as a giant ear of corn. "Since you're both altos."

"Thanks, Jenny," Anni said.

"Thanks, Jenny," Ed echoed. "Will I see you at rehearsal tomorrow?"

"For sure," the ear of corn said. "The holiday concert's my favorite!"

Larkin hadn't realized that the choir would continue singing, after performing the Beethoven—but of course it would, it wasn't like theater where you came together and disbanded after six weeks. A choir was different. More permanent. The kind of commitment that could change a life.

She wanted in.

"Why didn't I know there was rehearsal tomorrow? I swear, Ed, I read your emails."

"Because"—Anni, as usual, was quickest to the answer

—"you were on the megachoir email list and you aren't on the concert choir email list."

"Can I be?" Larkin turned to Ed; asked the question that would force him to say aloud what he thought, when he looked at her, even though she knew it was way too early to ask. "Would it be weird? If we were doing what we're doing now *and* I was singing in your choir? Is it against, like, the rules?"

"Of course not," Ed said, taking her hand and squeezing it. "Here, I'll make it official. Larkin Day, you are now a member of our concert choir. Will I see you at rehearsal tomorrow?"

Larkin leaned forward and kissed Ed's unmasked cheek. "Yes."

———

Want to read more? Join Larkin, Ed, Anni, the person who just sent Anni that mysterious email, Jo, Claire, and the rest of the gang in their next adventure — Like, Subscribe, and Murder!

AUTHOR'S NOTE

Last weekend we went to the lake again—Larry and me, for the first time this season.

Larry is the Great Love of My Life; you can read more about our love story in *What It Is and What to Do Next*.

Or you can read more about our love story in *What If It Were This*.

Or *Underground/Wonderland*.

We haven't decided what to call it yet; if we end up going with *Underground/Wonderland*, it will have to be typeset as *underGround/0nder1and* (since the zine is [in part] about Lewis Carroll and programming) and it could be more difficult to market—although I suspect I may have successfully marketed the zine to at least one of you (preferably the one who is reading this right now).

Where was I?

The lake.

It was at the lake, last year, that Larry asked me, "When are you going to write your next novel?"

He didn't actually phrase it that way—he would never say something quite so cliché, which is one of the reasons why we enjoy talking to each other so much (we are stereophones, not stereotypes).

What Larry said, in truth, was: "I think there is a little bit of you that is still missing, and we won't get to see it until you start writing fiction again."

What I said—and you'll have to believe that it happened *exactly like this*—was: "I can't believe you just said that. I mean, maybe I *can* believe it, if there's one thing you and I are good at it's seeing the truth about a thing, *what-it-is-ism*, and I was going to tell you if you hadn't brought it up yourself, that I had brought something to read to you."

"Ahhh," Larry said, in exactly the way you might imagine. "You're writing something new."

"Not exactly. It's just a few chapters of this mystery I started working on before the pandemic. You can tell me if I should keep going."

You already know what he told me.

If I wanted to market this book properly, I would end it with a scotcheroo recipe—but since my eating habits are much more akin to Anni's than Larkin's (which means that any scotcheroo instructions I include would be copy/pasted from the internet [and you can look those up on your own]), I want to end this author's note by *writing about writing*.

Specifically, I want to write about revision.

Some people claim that *writing is rewriting*, remarking with astonishment that they didn't even think of creating *this character* or *that subplot* until their third pass through the draft.

I'm an outliner (a plotter, in *plotter vs. pantser* parlance) which means that everything I want to put into my novels gets written down well in advance of what you might call the "actual writing" (it is, of course, all "actual writing"). I might not think of creating *this character* or *that subplot* until my third or fourth pass through the outline, but by the time I sit down to write the first chapter I know pretty much how the book is going to go—and if you were to read the first completed draft of *Ode to Murder,* you would note that it was pretty much the same as the one you just finished reading.

The interesting questions, therefore, become *what I decided to change* and *why I decided to change it.*

If you visit NicoleDieker.com and sign up for my mailing list, you'll get not only updates about the next Larkin Day mystery novel but also information about upcoming classes and public appearances. You'll also get the occasional writing-and-life insight that may inspire you to start working on your own series of books—or, at least, to continue reading mine.

Since you've already done the work of reading *this* book, I'll give you one of those insights right now. It can apply to both writing and life, if you choose.

Feeling bad is a sign that something needs to change.

When I revise my writing, I go through the document from beginning to end and ask myself what I might apologize for, if I were reading it aloud. Then I fix everything I feel badly about. This is something I learned as a pianist, after years of making excuses for problems I hadn't yet solved. "That's the hard part," I used to say—and it is! Fixing the stuff that makes you feel bad is *extremely difficult,* and it's much easier to ask for forgiveness instead of giving yourself the permission to make it better. "Sorry," we might say, "I know that's not my best work." Because, you know, *we know.*

Here, as an example, is the original beginning of the novel:

"I'm not going to choir practice tonight," Larkin told her mother.

"Yes, you are," Josephine Day said, not looking up from her laptop. "I already told Ed you'd be there."

"You can't tell people I'll be places," Larkin said, not getting up from the sofa. "That's not how this is going to work."

"I think I get at least some say in how it's going to work," Josephine said. "Since you are living in my house."

"Temporarily," Larkin said.

"I'm well aware."

"And I'm supposed to be taking some time off," Larkin continued, projecting her voice towards the kitchen table in the hopes that it would loom over her mother and withdraw with some sympathy extracted. "To think about what I want to do with the rest of my life."

"Are you thinking about it?"

"I'm thinking that I don't want to sing in community choir."

"It's not a community choir. We're bringing together all of the choruses in the Corridor for this concert." At least her mother had not called it the Creative Corridor this time, emphasis on *creative*, as if that would entice Larkin to get off the sofa and get back to creating. She did not want to make art in Iowa. Not in Iowa City; not in Dubuque, Des Moines, Davenport or any of the other towns they listed in *The Music Man*; and certainly not in Cedar Rapids.

The first fix—the easy one—was *The Music Man* reference. I knew the bit about Dubuque, Des Moines, Davenport and so on would get cut (in fact, I knew it *while I was in the process of writing it down*), although I left it as a place-holder until I finished the first draft and had enough brain-space to go back and give both *Larkin* and *my readers* something more interesting to think about.

When I read Larry my revised version, "She didn't want to make art in any city where you had to say the name of the state afterwards," he laughed out loud.

The harder fix was the sentence in which Larkin projects her voice. That sat in the draft until the very end, even though I knew it would need to change before I could publish. Every time I read "projecting her voice towards the kitchen table in the hopes that it would loom over her mother and withdraw with some sympathy extracted" I thought to myself *what does that even mean?* Voices can project, to be sure, but can they loom? Withdraw? Extract? That's a lot of stuff for a voice to do; it's also a lot of stuff for a reader to parse, and none of it quite makes sense together.

I originally wrote the sentence because I wanted to let the reader know, as quickly as possible, that Larkin was a theater person; that she not only knew how to project her voice and work towards an objective, but also that she thought of the world in these particular terms. I solved the problem once I realized that the more important piece of information for the reader, at this time in the novel, was that Larkin was a person who had gone stagnant. That's the conflict, in this first conversation—whether Larkin will follow her mother's instructions and *do something*, or whether she will continue to sit on her mother's sofa and *do nothing*.

That gave me this:

"And I'm supposed to be taking some time off," Larkin continued, shifting position just enough to activate her core and project her voice towards the kitchen table. "To think about what I want to do with the rest of my life."

"Are you thinking about it?"

"I'm thinking that I don't want to sing in community choir." Larkin was actually thinking that it had been a very long time since she had activated her core.

Writing may be *rewriting,* as the cliché would have you believe; I prefer to think of it as *resolving,* a word that is both a triple entendre and a triple threat. All three meanings apply, in the case of you and your work—the resolve, the re-solving, and the resolution.

Examples are necessary, as Larry once wrote me (you'll be able to read his entire letter in the first volume of our zine) and so I will give you one more.

If you've taken the time to browse the Shortwave Media catalog, you might have seen Shortwave founder Alan Lastufka's debut novel *Face the Night.* You might even have bought a copy; if you haven't, I'm going to spend the next three paragraphs selling it to you.

I read an early draft of *Face the Night* in 2018; when I read the final draft in 2022, I was delighted by all of the ways in which the text had been subtly improved. I can't speak to Alan's revision process—you'll have to visit AlanLastufka.com and sign up for his newsletter for that—but I can speak to the results.

Here's the first paragraph, as it was in the version Alan sent me that summer:

Adriana mentally ticked off all of the things she'd let herself forget in just the last three years. The little things she noticed again now. Like the way his lips held a cigarette limp until he would laugh and it'd shoot straight up threatening to burn his cheek. Or the way his dirty crew socks always frayed around his long second toe. Or just how much he bled when she stuck him.

Here's the same paragraph, in the version you're going to start reading later today:

Adriana mentally ticked off all the things she'd let herself forget over the last three years. Like the way his lips held a cigarette, limp, until he laughed and it shot straight up, threatening to burn his cheek. Or his dirty crew socks, always frayed around his long second toe. Or just how much he bled when she stuck him.

I teach writing, and I could teach a 90-minute class on those two paragraphs. However, I secretly believe that people learn best when they work things out on their own (I'm also terrible at keeping secrets) so I'm going to let you have the fun of finding the differences between them.

Then I'm going to let you do the work of figuring out how each of those differences—each of Alan's *revisions*—improves the opening chapter of *Face the Night*. What did Alan change, and why did he change it? If you would like to email either me or Alan to let us know what you came up with, I'll let you know in advance that you'll have to come up with something better than "it's just better." *Face the Night* just won the 2022 Hoffer Award for Best Commercial Fiction, after all.

On the subject of email, Alan has just emailed me—the programming-and-philosophy zine, which you can also purchase through Shortwave Media, has both a cover and a title: *What It Is and What to Do Next*.

We have work to do. See you next book.

—Nicole Dieker, May 2022

ACKNOWLEDGMENTS

Thanks to Shortwave Media for seeing the potential in this series.

Thanks to Alan Lastufka for turning *Ode to Murder* from a double-spaced document into a beautifully designed book.

Thanks to Erin Foster for proofreading the final draft and finding one continuity error that no one else noticed.

Thanks to Joe and Mary Dieker, Julie Kraft, and Chris Solaro for reading early drafts and sharing their thoughts.

Thanks to Larry Finley for listening to me read the entire first draft aloud, chapter by chapter, including all of the parts where I said "wait, this could be clearer" or "wait, I just used that word twice" or "wait, you aren't supposed to know that part yet" and paused the reading to revise the previous sentence.

Thanks to you for reading all the way to the end.

I hope you'll read the next one.

ABOUT THE AUTHOR

Nicole Dieker is a writer, teacher, and musician. She began her writing career as a full-time freelancer with a focus on personal finance and habit formation; she launched her fiction career with *The Biographies of Ordinary People*, a definitely-not-autobiographical novel that follows three sisters from 1989 to 2016.

Currently, Dieker writes the *Larkin Day* mystery series and the perzine *WHAT IT IS and WHAT TO DO NEXT*. She also maintains an active freelance career; her work has appeared in Vox, Morning Brew, Lifehacker, Bankrate, Haven Life, Popular Science, and more. Dieker spent five years as writer and editor for The Billfold, a personal finance blog where people had honest conversations about money.

Praise from Kirkus Reviews: "Dieker excels at depicting how real people think and act."

Dieker lives in Quincy, Illinois with the great love of her life, his piano, and their garden.

www.ingramcontent.com/pod-product-compliance
Lightning Source LLC
Chambersburg PA
CBHW021321190726
48288CB00003B/903